PRAISE FOR THE FIERY TALES

"Evocative, erotic. . . [A] sensual treat!"
— **Sylvia Day**,
#1 *New York Times* bestselling author

"Hot enough to warm the coldest winter night."
— **Publishers Weekly**

"Sophisticated and deeply romantic."
—**Elizabeth Hoyt**,
New York Times bestselling author

"Sure to delight!"
— **Jennifer Ashley**,
New York Times bestselling author

"The most luscious, sexy take on classic fairy tales I've ever read!"
—**Cheryl Holt**,
New York Times bestselling author

"Sets the classic fairy tale(s) ablaze!"
—**Anna Campbell**,
bestselling, award-winning author

Bewitching in Boots

A Fiery Tale

LILA DIPASQUA

DiPasqua

PRINTING HISTORY
First Edition: From *Awakened by a Kiss*, Berkley Sensation/Penguin Group (USA) Inc.—August 2010

Second Edition: Lila DiPasqua—June 2016
ISBN: 978-0-9951655-1-9 (trade pbk)
ISBN: 978-0-9951655-0-2 (e-book)

To Bruno, who has always been there for me.
You're the best brother.
Ever.

BEWITCHING IN BOOTS

Moral of the Story of Puss in Boots:

"If a man has quick success
In winning such a fair princess,
By turning on the charm,
Then regard his manners, looks, and dress,
That inspired her deepest tenderness,
For they can't do one any harm."

Charles Perrault (1628–1703)

CHAPTER ONE

France 1685

"Do you *really* think your plan will work, Elisabeth?" Claire swiped a curl from her damp forehead. The summer breeze stealing its way into their moving carriage was a mixed blessing. It offered some relief from the heat, but brought with it wafts of dust.

This wasn't the most comfortable trip Elisabeth de Roussel had ever taken, but it was the most important—to her. "For the third time, yes." Her voice was calm, belying the disquiet she felt. Her nerves jangled; she didn't need her sister to keep repeating the same question.

"You're going to seduce Tristan de Tiersonnier, a man who makes other men quake with fear and women tremble with desire. And you're going to do it, dressed like *that?*"

"That is the plan." Elisabeth glanced over at her maid, Agathe, and caught her rolling her eyes. Elisabeth fully expected the older woman to voice her dissent over the plan, but instead Agathe was uncharacteristically quiet, and stared out the window, lips pursed.

Claire leaned in. "Elisabeth, you are dressed like a *man*. A shirt, breeches, black boots—those are men's clothes. Well, perhaps not *those* black boots. No man would wear something so snug around his calves."

"I'm quite aware of how I'm dressed, dear sister." Her younger sibling didn't need to know what an utter mess Elisabeth was inside. Nor was she going to admit that she was dressed this way because she wanted—needed—her prized sword at her hip. It gave her confidence. Helped to bolster courage. And courage was what she'd need to execute her plan.

Especially when the plan centered on the only man who intimidated her. The imposing sinfully beautiful former commander of the King's private Guard—the Musketeers—Tristan de Tiersonnier, Comte de Saint-Marcel.

One look from his intense blue eyes and she was undone—when no man shook her, not even her father, the King. By doing nothing more than walking into a room, Tristan commanded her attention and ignited her senses—reducing her into some gawking unsophisticated ingénue. With his confident manner, his tall and powerful body, he exuded authority. And—God help her—such potent sensuality. He made her ache. Heart and body.

He burned in her blood.

Sadly, nothing had lessened her fever for Tristan. Not marriage to another man. Not the lovers she'd taken since the Duc's death. Not time or distance.

"I'm all for being a part of your plan, Elisabeth," Claire said. "In fact, I'd never refuse. But this one is rather involved."

That was an understatement.

Claire had no idea just how involved her plan was or what Elisabeth truly hoped to accomplish during this sojourn, but she couldn't explain all of it to her sister. Claire always looked up to her. As much as she adored Claire, Elisabeth couldn't reveal to her, or anyone, just how vulnerable she was to Tristan.

It was a weakness. She never showed her weaknesses. One didn't survive in her world by being transparent—ever.

And Elisabeth had survived plenty of attempts to diminish her, both at court and in the eyes of the King. Her late mother had taught her well. She'd been a fine example of how strength and a cunning mind benefited a woman. Her mother hadn't kept the King's interest longer than any of his other mistresses without knowing a thing or two about how to be clever in a man's world. Elisabeth had adopted her mother's finesse and fortitude and had risen among the brood sired by His Majesty to become the favorite royal daughter. And she used her favored position to protect Claire—who went mostly unnoticed and unprotected by their father— from the constant courtly intrigue.

"*Hrrmph* . . . Seems like a lot of trouble to go to just to bed a man," Agathe mumbled. "We could have stayed home. There are plenty of men at Versailles to choose from."

"There are indeed," Elisabeth said. Her period of mourning over, during the last year she'd had her choice of lovers. Had the freedom to pick and choose whom she wanted. She'd enjoyed the freedom that came with widowhood.

But her freedom was running out.

If she was going to do something about Tristan, it had to be *now*.

"The men at court bore me," Elisabeth added, affecting a tone that was purposely blasé. One that gave the world the impression she was indifferent to all things. "The timing is perfect. Veronique is no longer Tristan's mistress. This is the most opportune time."

Claire crinkled her nose. "Veronique . . ." she muttered with disdain. A disdain shared by Elisabeth for their unscrupulous half-sister, the court filled with too many just like her.

"Opportune time?" Agathe snorted. "Perhaps madame has forgotten that the man was dismissed from his position as Captain of the Guard—and the reason why?"

"I haven't forgotten, Agathe," Elisabeth said, "and it is not a permanent situation. Tristan is strong and skilled. Sooner or later His Majesty will reinstate him." She'd see to it. It was part of her plan, important for many reasons, including thwarting Veronique's ambitions. Three months ago, Tristan had been injured in the line of duty. For two months he'd convalesced at the palace until the King, acting on the advice of the royal physicians who felt Tristan would never completely heal, had replaced him as Captain of the Guard.

"So how do you plan on seducing him?" Claire asked, her eyes twinkling with mischief.

Elisabeth smiled. "Now where would be the fun in telling you that? You'll just have to wait and see." She had no idea how she was going to go about seducing Tristan. Her mother had taught her how to entice men, what they liked in and out of the boudoir. But Tristan was not like any man she'd ever known. He wasn't the sort of man who could be led around by the nose. He wouldn't be easily lured.

Claire frowned. "I will still get to help you, yes?"

"Of course. That's why I brought you along." Elisabeth glanced at Agathe. "I'm going to need both of you to help."

Her old and faithful servant looked about as thrilled over the prospect as she'd be at developing a body rash.

"Excellent." Claire beamed. "I do so admire your bravery, Elisabeth. Normally women wait to be approached by Tristan de Tiersonnier. You're the only woman I know who is willing to approach him. He's a little too serious, a little too intense for me. I've always found him to be rather unnerving."

So did she. For entirely different reasons: the unbreakable pull he had on her and the desire she had for him that was far too keen. *If all goes well, you might have him tonight . . .* Her nerve endings quivered with life, the notion as thrilling as it was terrifying. It took all she possessed not to abort her plan and race back to Versailles. But she couldn't. Wouldn't. It was time to take control and sate the tormenting carnal hunger she had for this man—who'd barely noticed her and had only spoken to her out of duty.

Well, today he'd notice her.

Acting on the signs she'd read in her father, on the subtle comments he'd made, Elisabeth knew he'd select a new husband for her soon. She'd be trapped in another hollow marriage filled with lonely nights fantasizing about Tristan. More lonely years spent starved for his touch, his taste.

She wouldn't go through that again.

If she was going to be forced to marry once more, then her husband may as well be Tristan. A husband of her choosing. If she failed to seduce him into the idea of marriage, then at the very least she wouldn't fail to seduce him into her bed for a week of unbridled sex. It was unwise, utterly foolhardy, for a woman to crave a man as intensely as she craved Tristan. To be as spellbound as she was by him. Her mother had taught her better than that. One way or another, husband or lover, he'd bed her and she'd at last satisfy this hunger, snap this fascination, and purge him from her heart, body and soul.

She'd never find any contentment in her life—know any peace—if she didn't break the power Tristan had over her.

"I find Tiersonnier appealing," Elisabeth remarked. "And as for his 'intensity,' I think that could be put to good use in the boudoir."

Claire giggled. "Too true, sister."

Agathe pursed her lips firmer together.

Elisabeth's plan was simple. Before she could marry Tristan, she had to convince both the King and Tristan that the irresistible ex-Musketeer was her perfect match.

There were only two problems with her plan. One, the King saw Tristan as infirm and not fit to marry her. And two, Tristan wasn't going be easy to seduce into her bed, much less into marriage.

He hated her.

The carriage stopped. Her entourage of Musketeers and a second carriage filled with Elisabeth's and Claire's trunks and necessities halted as well.

Elisabeth alighted from the carriage with the help of one of the King's Guardsmen. Her stomach dropped at the sight before her.

"Good Lord, Elisabeth, is that Tiersonnier's château?" her sister asked, stopping by her side.

Agathe simply shook her head in dismay.

Standing in the courtyard, overgrown with weeds, was an old two-story country mansion, its stone masonry crumbling in many spots. The once proud mythical statues adorning its rooftops were blackened with dirt and age.

Elisabeth took a deep breath and let it out slowly. "It's in some need of repair."

Agathe snorted. "That is putting it mildly."

This isn't a setback. She wasn't going to be discouraged by the state of Tristan's abode or, more important, what it suggested about the finances of the lord of this château and how that diminished her already slim chances of being with Tristan beyond the week. She'd come this far. She'd forge ahead.

She'd simply add to the plan. What was one more obstacle in her path? After all, she was already attempting the impossible. In addition to convincing the King that Tristan was capable of commanding His Majesty's Guard once more, and making Tristan want her, clearly she'd have to convince her father that Tristan was richer than he was.

She was wearing her lucky boots. Good thing.

She was going to need all the luck she could get.

*****

"Is this what you do all day? Sit in the library?" Gabriel de Tiersonnier asked with a smile as he strolled into the room.

Seated on the settee, his leg propped up, Tristan stared out at the gardens. Without glancing at his brother, he responded dryly, "No. Sometimes I sit in the salon." His tone was caustic. Embittered.

He wanted to be left alone and tried to ignore his younger brother and his good mood. It was as infuriating as the unrelenting dull ache in Tristan's leg. An incessant reminder of his debilitated state. All these weeks and no bloody sign of improvement. He still walked with a cane. He still couldn't make peace with his crippled limb. He hadn't wanted to believe the royal physicians' prognosis. Now he was beginning to lose all hope of a complete recovery.

And his frustration and fury over it mounted daily.

Still smiling, Gabriel shook his head and sat down in a nearby chair, making himself comfortable.

Merde. His brother meant to stay.

"Really, Tristan, this sedate existence of yours is as exciting as living among celibate monks."

"You should know. You were one of them—that is until they tossed you out last week." Gabriel had returned two days ago, shattering Tristan's solitude, and he resented it.

He resented just about everything nowadays. He resented how far he'd fallen for a man who had it all—command of the most prestigious, most elite corps in the realm, the ear of the King and his esteem, magnificent apartments at Versailles, and a number of women to bed whenever he chose, including his favorite, Veronique. But his favorite turned out to be a conniving little opportunist, who was quick to leave. The moment he was replaced as Captain of the Musketeers, she was bedding his successor.

What did he have left when all the dust had settled? A lame leg. A broken-down château he cared nothing about. And worse, staid empty years stretched out before him—a life so contrary to his active existence. He'd fought in countless campaigns for his country during his distinguished military career. He'd risen through the ranks to eventually head the King's private Guard, and had conducted covert operations and quashed conspiracies while in charge of the safety and protection of the royal family.

Gabriel chuckled good-naturedly. "I was not a monk, and well you know it. I was in the seminary. I hadn't taken any vows yet. Our dear departed father felt he needed to have one son in the service of God. I told him it was a mistake to send me."

"I suppose 'our dear departed father' overestimated your restraint. Here you thought celibacy was a mere suggestion and not a requirement for a man studying to become a member of the Holy Church."

"Exactly." Gabriel grinned. "Glad you see my point."

"Yes, and who could have guessed they'd take it so seriously when they caught you with two women at the same time—twice."

Gabriel laughed. "Ah, now Tristan, those women were well worth being expelled from the seminary. Who needs to wait to die to go to paradise when a man can sample those four lovelies right here on earth?"

"Tristan?" The sound of his uncle's voice grabbed Tristan's attention. He turned to see Richard de Tiersonnier entered the room, his brow furrowed. Despite his salt and pepper hair, he was still the tall, strong figure he'd been during his years in the military. "Are you expecting a Duc?"

"A *Duc?*" Tristan repeated. "Of course not, why?" No one from court had visited him since his departure from the royal palace. He'd been well forgotten in mere weeks—after years of loyal service to the King and his family.

"There is a six-horse carriage among the entourage outside."

Tristan was baffled. *Entourage?* A six-horse carriage was definitely a Duc. What Duc? Why was he here?

Grabbing his cane, he struggled to his feet, refusing help from Gabriel, and made his way to the courtyard to greet his notable visitor, his uncle and brother falling in behind him.

The moment Tristan stepped outside the main entrance of his château, he arrested his steps. His heart lost a beat. Two carriages, one with six white horses, and thirty of his former men each on horseback filled his courtyard.

But if that wasn't enough, by far the most astonishing sight was the King's favorite daughter, Elisabeth, Duchesse de Roussel. Flanked by her maid and her sister, she stood not twenty feet away dressed in breeches, black boots and a white shirt—male clothing custom-fitted to her form.

She looked like anything but a man.

Her breeches accentuated her mouth-watering curves, black boots—like none he'd ever seen—molded to her slender calves, and then there was her shirt. The breeze fluttered the white material, teasing him with glimpses of creamy skin above her breasts. He felt his prick harden.

Tristan squeezed the handle of his cane. *Jésus-Christ*, he hadn't had sex since his injury. He'd definitely gone too long without a good fuck if the sight of the King's most spoiled offspring, dressed in men's clothing, was stiffening his cock.

"Where is the Duc?" his uncle asked.

Gabriel stepped around Tristan. "Never mind that, Uncle. Who is that woman dressed in breeches?"

"One of His Majesty's illegitimate daughters." Tristan couldn't keep the disdain from his tone.

"I thought he legitimized all his children born to his mistresses," Richard stated.

"He did. He gave them status and arranged powerful matches for them, too," Tristan said. "This is one of the more self-indulgent among those in the royal brood."

Tightening his jaw, he made his way across the courtyard, hating it that his former men had to see him hobbling like a cripple. Whatever Elisabeth wanted, he'd refuse. Whatever game she was playing—and it was obvious she was up to no good—he wouldn't engage in it.

He was going to send her and her entourage straight back to Versailles.

CHAPTER TWO

Elisabeth's heart hammered in her chest as she watched Tristan approach. He wasn't happy to see her. No surprise there. The summer wind caressed his dark hair and pressed his shirt against his strong chest. Normally in uniform, this was the first time she'd ever seen him in plain clothing.

He looked even more dangerous and delicious.

Elisabeth felt the usual hot quickening in her belly at the sight of him.

He stopped, towering before her, and gave a short stiff obligatory bow. "Madame, to what do I owe this honor?" The last word was particularly weighty with sarcasm.

Here we go, Elisabeth . . . She prayed he didn't notice how she trembled. Schooling her features, she lifted her chin a notch. "And a good day to you, too, Tristan." She'd never addressed him in such a familiar manner, but if she wanted a more intimate involvement, she might as well speak to him in a more intimate way. "Yes, I am well and I had a good trip. Thank you." She kept her tone light and her gaze fixed to his, anxiety and arousal swirling through her system. Just being this close to him made her sex moisten.

His eyes narrowed slightly. "Forgive my manners." His reply was tightly dealt. "I should have inquired about your well-being and your trip. I'm glad all is well. The point of your visit is?"

The man didn't believe in mincing words, did he? He couldn't make it more obvious he wanted her gone. Posthaste. Well, she wasn't going anywhere.

"Agathe, the letter, please." She held out her hand to her maid.

Agathe handed her the folded parchment she'd been entrusted with.

Elisabeth held it out to Tristan. "From the King."

Taking the letter from her, Tristan broke open the seal with one hand, leaning heavily on his cane with the other, and scanned its contents. He snorted. "This asks that I help you secure a new fencing instructor."

"That's correct." Every so often the breeze blew just the right way and delighted her senses with his scent. He smelled wonderful. All male. Potent and virile, his leg injury diminishing him in no way in her eyes. She wanted to lean in and inhale deeply, and had to fight back the urge to lace her arms around him and brush her lips along his neck, his skin tempting her in the worst way. Too many nights she'd lain in bed, wondering how he'd feel against her, inside her. Her every instinct told her that any amorous encounter with this man would be like none she'd ever known. Behind the cold glares he gave her was a man who was naturally—deliciously—dominant in the boudoir. With a wicked blend of hot sensuality and sinful skills, he knew how to drive a woman wild. Stories of his sexual talents abounded at the palace.

Sadly, he didn't even need to lift a finger to affect her. She was already wild and wet for him.

"I'll be staying awhile. We all will." She gestured toward the large group she'd brought. "Now if you will show me to my rooms."

Gripped by anger, his light blue eyes shone with such bedazzling fire.

"Duchesse, I'll not show you anywhere, except back to your carriage. I have no fencing instructor to suggest to you. Inform the King of my regrets. Kindly take your party and return to Versailles."

Where most would have stepped back when on the receiving end of one of Tristan de Tiersonnier's fierce looks and sharp tones, boldly she took a step closer to him. A delectable rush of heat flooded over her. Her nipples tightened and pressed hard against her shirt.

"I don't think so. I am staying." She forced herself to hold his regard without wavering. "You see, my father knows how much I love to fence and has always provided me with fine instructors in the past. I've learned all I can from my last instructor. Therefore, I need a new one. He has ordered you to assist me in finding one to my liking, and I've chosen the instructor I want. *You*."

Tristan gave a harsh laugh. "*Me?* Madame, are you blind? Perhaps you missed my injured leg?" he all but growled at her.

Unfazed, she responded, "I'm aware of your injury. It won't hinder you, I'm sure. You are the best swordsman in the country. You have a lot to teach me. And you'll not disobey your King's orders."

She stepped around him. Without turning back, she walked toward the château with purposeful strides, passing the small group of servants who'd formed a line outside, her sister and maid on her heels. She hated sounding spoiled and demanding, knowing it fed into his preconceived notions of her, but he left her no choice. He needed persuasion. Only by throwing the King's name and authority around could she bend his will to hers.

"Oh, this is good. This is so much better than the seminary." Gabriel snickered. "Tristan, I don't believe I've ever seen a woman order you about."

Tristan watched the saucy sway of Elisabeth's luscious derrière as she walked away. He held back the expletives bellowing in his head. He was at a full cock stand—in front of a fucking squad of his former men. In fact, the moment she'd stepped close and he'd noticed the telltale sign of her pebbled nipples, he was slammed with a hot wave of arousal. He was exciting her. *Merde*. It was affecting him.

He didn't need this. He was already in torment thanks to his leg. He didn't need his prick to add to his misery. Elisabeth de Roussel was nothing more than a coquette—a flirt who didn't offer up the ultimate prize. He'd seen her cock-teasing at court. She had it down to an art. With her beauty and wit, she had men all but panting for her. She lapped it up, purring with pleasure over their interest and thriving on the power she wielded over them. Countless fools had vied for her attention and were ultimately turned down.

Few had ever made it to her bed. It was a game to her. A mere diversion.

The royal family was, by and large, self-absorbed and full of artifice—Veronique and Elisabeth among the worst. Only Veronique never received preferential treatment from the King the way Elisabeth did. Loyalty, honesty and honor meant nothing to any member of His Majesty's family. Not a sincere soul in the bunch. He didn't miss the games at court or those who played them.

Clearly, Elisabeth was bored, looking for new diversions.

He wasn't about to become that diversion.

Tristan glanced at the men he used to command. Most were dismounting and wouldn't make eye contact with him. Their first meeting since his dismissal, the awkwardness and tension in the air was palpable. He missed leading these men. Every one of the twenty-seven hundred that made up the King's private Guard was of noble birth, impeccable character, and superior skill. If he were still in charge, he could order them to escort the Duchesse de Roussel back to the palace with a letter to the King recommending that for her own safety his daughter not travel the countryside in her outrageous attire. But he had no authority over them any longer. They had to abide by their mistress's wishes, unable to take orders from him.

"Tristan, what do you wish to do with all these men?" Richard asked.

Out of the corner of his eye he could see Gabriel grinning, thoroughly enjoying himself.

"Send them to the stables until I settle this matter."

They wouldn't be there long.

She was leaving.

*****

She wasn't leaving, she told herself. *You are going to collect yourself and not allow him to overwhelm you. Not with his size. Not with his scratchy temperament, and most especially not with his potent allure.* It was bad enough she was having a difficult time thinking clearly with him near, her thoughts dominated by the shameless fantasies he inspired.

"Well, at least the inside of the château looks better than the outside," Agathe remarked, glancing around. Standing in the vestibule, Elisabeth gazed up at the grand staircase, caring little about the condition of Tristan's home at the moment. Not when she needed to steel her resolve so that she didn't run back to Versailles like a coward. In a few moments, Tristan would enter the château and she had to be ready for another round of wits and wills.

She was supposed to be seducing him. Have him mindless with hunger for her. She thought she'd seen heated interest in his eyes. Or was that simply wishful thinking? Her senses were so frenzied, she couldn't say for certain if she was having a warming effect on him—beyond anger.

Claire placed her hand on Elisabeth's shoulder. "Are you all right? You look a bit flushed."

Elisabeth forced a smile. "It's this terrible heat. I'm fine." Nothing could be further from the truth. She was in over her head and drowning fast.

Tristan entered with the same two men who'd been with him outside, both men bearing a striking resemblance to him, though one gentleman was at least twenty-five years Tristan's senior.

The second Tristan spotted her in the grand entranceway, he marched to her, his cane aiding him along.

Anytime he entered a room, his male beauty took her breath away. Now was no exception. Her breath stuck in her throat for a moment and her heart gave a flutter.

Oh, Elisabeth, you are so under his spell. She was all but ready to throw herself at him and beg him to take her just so she'd have some relief from the yearning throbbing through her core. Anything that would put an end to this attraction and affinity.

She dropped her gaze briefly and couldn't help but notice the pronounced bulge in his breeches. Dear God, he . . . desired her! It was indisputable. It was incredible.

A sudden surge of much-needed confidence welled inside her. Her insides danced.

Frowning, he halted before her.

Smiling, she looked up at him. *Oh, yes . . . This is going to happen.* He was going to be her lover. *Maybe even more . . .* her heart whispered.

"I don't know what game you are playing, Duchesse. Nor do I wish to know," he said. "If you're looking for new forms of amusement, I suggest you seek them out at court. Not here."

"Please excuse my brother. He has completely forgotten his manners, madame." The younger man elbowed past his older sibling. He had the same dark hair, but his eyes were not as vibrant as Tristan's blue eyes. "Allow me to introduce myself. I'm Gabriel de Tiersonnier." He took her hand and pressed a kiss to it. "This is our uncle, Richard de Tiersonnier."

The older gentleman stepped forward and kissed her hand, too. "*Enchanté*, madame."

"A pleasure to meet you both." She introduced her sister. Her nerves were beginning to settle as she became surer of herself. If Tristan desired her, even a little, she had him.

Tristan simply glowered silently at her, then reluctantly murmured an apology and a greeting to Claire.

"Now then, about my lessons." Elisabeth leaped back into the subject before Tristan could begin a new tirade. She stepped close to Tristan again, this time leaving less room between their bodies than she had outside. Something flared in his eyes, something she read as hunger.

Her fever spiked.

Praying he couldn't tell just how undone she was by him, lest she lose ground, she managed to state firmly, "You'll provide a lesson every day. First thing in the morning. You see, I've challenged someone. By week's end, I expect, thanks to your instructions, to be able to best him."

He held her stare for a moment. "Whom have you challenged?" There was skepticism in his tone. He thought she was lying. Well, she was lying. Normally, she didn't give a whit what people thought of her. Would she have taken up fencing if she had? But Tristan's low opinion of her bothered her.

Had always bothered her.

"That is none of your concern. You'll be paid generously for your time and skill."

"Madame. . . ." he began, his voice low and thick with ire.

"Please call me Elisabeth."

"Madame," he repeated, this time sharply. The man was beyond stubborn. "If I cannot command the Musketeers, I most certainly am not fit to be your instructor—the King will quite agree with me." Each word was laced with bitterness. She couldn't blame him for being bitter. Elisabeth hated how quickly her father had dismissed and replaced Tristan. His years of devoted service completely ignored. That his injury had occurred during an assassin's attempt against the King, Tristan saving his life, had been seemingly inconsequential to her father. "Get back in the carriage and return to your palace. Your father—"

"Was right to send you here," Gabriel injected. "Tristan *is* the best swordsman in the realm. And of course, we wouldn't want to offend the King, now would we, Tristan?" He patted his shoulder. "You and your lovely sister are most welcome." Gabriel smiled.

Tristan dragged his gaze away from Elisabeth to give his brother a murderous glare.

Gabriel's brows shot up. "*What?* It's but a week. Only seven days. A flash of time, then it's over." Gabriel glanced at Claire then back to Elisabeth, his smile returning. "Such a short time to spend in such charming company."

"I agree with Gabriel," Richard said. His uncle was a man of few words. This was a fine time for him to start voicing his opinion. "You are most welcome to stay . . . and if you change your mind and want a different fencing instructor, you may look to me, madame. I taught Tristan everything he knows."

Tristan strived for patience. His uncle and brother didn't know what kind of woman they were dealing with—although her mode of dress should have alerted them to the obvious— she was trouble. Willful. Acting as though society's mores didn't apply to her because she was the King's favorite daughter. A week with Elisabeth running about in her tight-fitted stirring attire. Of her trying to garner the very physical reactions she'd wrought from his unruly cock.

Christ, of her entertaining herself at his expense.

It wasn't going to happen.

Yet, if she wished to stay, he couldn't toss her out—just as she'd gleefully pointed out. He may not be in His Majesty's employ any longer, but was still obliged to his King. And he had to oblige the King's favorite daughter, because of it.

However, the key here was *if* she wished to stay.

This was his home. His domain she was under. And there were a number of highly appealing ideas flitting through his mind on how to sway her into wanting to leave and abandon the fencing lessons she was demanding.

For the first time since she'd arrived, he found himself fighting back a smile.

"Are you sure you'd be comfortable staying here for these lessons, madame?" he asked. "This isn't Versailles."

She smiled at him, though it didn't reach her large hazel eyes. "I'll manage," she said tightly. For the first time he saw a break in her façade. He'd irked her. She didn't like his comment that suggested she was pampered. Odd. Why would the obvious annoy her?

"I'd like to refresh myself now. Could you order me a bath?" Elisabeth's features were schooled once again, and she was speaking as though the matter were settled. As if there were never any doubt he'd comply with her demands.

Normally he'd be vexed, but he wasn't, not while plans were taking shape in his mind. By the time he was through with her, she'd bend to *his* will. And leave, taking his former men with her.

"Of course," Tristan ceded, and caught the surprised looks on his brother's and uncle's faces. Tristan called to his majordomo standing in the vestibule. "Please escort our guests upstairs to the east wing."

"The *east* wing?" Gabriel said. "But, Tristan—"

"The. East. Wing." Tristan gave his brother a look of warning, silently ordering him to hold his tongue.

Once the women were upstairs, Gabriel didn't waste any time in questioning his decision. "Why did you give them rooms there? In the summer those rooms hardly get any breeze at all. They're terribly hot."

Richard shook his head. "That is exactly why he chose them, isn't it, Tristan?"

"Precisely. I want them gone. The sooner the better. I don't want to be responsible for any more of the royal brats. Especially Elisabeth de Roussel. She'll be uncomfortable and she'll flee for the palace."

It was Gabriel's turn to shake his head. "Brother, you are daft. She is beautiful, and in case you missed the way she looked at you, she's all but begging you to fuck her. How could you have missed the signs?"

"I missed nothing, Gabriel. She's not begging for anything of the sort. She's flirtatious with no intent on carrying through with an amorous encounter. It is nothing more than a coquettish act. One I've seen her play many times."

"Oh," Gabriel said, clearly disappointed. "Are you sure, Tristan? She certainly looked as though she'd be willing . . ." Clearly, his brother didn't want to let this go.

"She's not. And even if she were, I am not fucking the King's daughter."

"Why not? You bedded Veronique."

"Veronique is not the King's favorite daughter. Elisabeth is. And she holds no appeal for me." *Liar.* His stiffened cock proved otherwise. Before she put him through any more discomfort, he was getting rid of her.

There were a number of ways to chase her away. If the hot rooms didn't work, he could start responding to her sexual attempts. In fact, the more he thought about it, the more appeal it held for him.

He just might teach her a lesson on the folly of arousing sexual interest with no intention of finishing what she started.

"She'll be here a day, two at most."

She wouldn't last the week.

CHAPTER THREE

Elisabeth was miserable. It was early in the morning, the sun still new in the sky. Waiting for Tristan and her first lesson, she stood in the gardens—if the weed-ridden expanse littered with poorly tended shrubs and bushes could be considered a garden. Her scabbard rested against her hip, her precious sword sheathed within.

He was late.

She was exhausted.

She hadn't slept at all last night. Tossing and turning in her bed, thoughts of Tristan, images of his aroused body warming her, added to the heat in the stifling rooms. In fact, she suspected that if she'd slept in the kitchens near the cooking fires, she'd have been more comfortable.

She was no fool. It didn't take long for her to realize he'd selected the "east wing" for a reason. To make her stay as uncomfortable as possible so that she'd pack her trunks and return home. Elisabeth was willing to wager the other rooms at the opposite end of the château were much cooler.

Yesterday, she'd bathed. She'd primped. Spent the better part of the afternoon preparing for supper and had donned one of her favorite and most becoming gowns. With her pulse racing with nervous excitement, she'd made her way to the *Salle de Buffet* with Claire, only to find Richard and Gabriel there.

But no Tristan.

Gabriel had offered Tristan's apologies, claiming that his leg was troubling him. But she didn't believe it. She was troubling him. He was avoiding her.

And if he was avoiding her, then she was affecting him strongly. Good.

That made the time she spent with him during the fencing instruction all the more important to advancing her plan.

From the moment she'd laid eyes on him years ago, she'd been hopelessly enchanted. Other men paled in comparison. She'd tried not to look his way at the palace. She tried not to think of him. She'd tried to silence the errant emotions her heart had attached to him.

She'd failed.

This was her final opportunity to quell this infatuation.

The sooner he bedded her and diminished his hold on her, the better.

Then, if she succeeded in marrying Tristan, she'd have the civilized marriage she'd always wanted to a husband she respected and shared common interests with, like fencing— without the unsettling influence he presently had on her.

The sound of footsteps snatched her out of her thoughts. She snapped her head up and saw Tristan approaching, cane in hand, his baldric across his chest. He looked strong, despite the cane. And fierce. A formidable opponent on any battlefield, she often heard others say. He was well respected by his men. Admired by the realm. A highly decorated officer, his valor in battle was legendary.

His tan-colored breeches outlined his powerful thighs, his plain white shirt hung loosely from his broad shoulders, yet she could still detect the dips and ripples of his chiseled chest. A tiny thrill shivered down her spine when he stopped before her.

He looked so good, it made her ache.

"Good morning, Tristan." She smiled.

"Let's begin." Again no mincing of words. No exchange of pleasantries. She tamped down her irritation. Would it kill him to be less abrasive?

He unsheathed his sword. "I trust you know the basics?"

She knew more than the basics. Her passion for fencing was great. As a young girl, she'd watched the Musketeers practice as often as she could sneak away. Whenever they entertained the court with demonstrations of their skills, she'd been transfixed. It had taken carefully planned, carefully worded conversations with the King over a period of months before she'd finally managed to secure her first fencing instructor. That was years ago. Prior to her marriage. She still fenced. Still took it seriously. Practiced every opportunity she could.

She'd become so good at swords, she'd bested all of her instructors.

She was about to impress Tristan at last. Perhaps even garner herself a bit of praise for her skill and elevate his opinion of her.

"I'm no novice at swords." She unsheathed her blade and squeezed the hilt. She felt strong and it felt so right in her hand.

"Good. Then show me what you know. Step back and begin when you're ready."

She was smiling now as she assumed the proper stance. *"En garde."* She lunged at him on the attack.

His arm whipped up, his blade striking hers with stunning intensity, his defensive move ripping the hilt from her hand, sending her sword spiraling in the air before it landed twenty feet away with a *thump* in the weeds.

Her mouth agape, her palm throbbing, she simply blinked at him, astounded, reeling over how easily he'd just disarmed her.

Calmly, he sheathed his sword and stepped close to her, a mimic of what she'd done to him yesterday. Slipping his fingers under her chin, he tilted her head back, bringing her mouth within inches of his. For a moment, she forgot to breathe.

"Lesson one." His warm breath caressed her lips. "If you are going to engage in a sword fight, hold on to your sword."

He released her and walked away.

Her chin nearly collided with the ground in open-mouthed astonishment. Ire erupted inside her. She clamped her mouth shut and raced up to him, jumping in the way of his path, halting him in his tracks, her fists clenched at her sides.

"What was that?" she demanded.

He cocked a brow. "What was *what?*"

"That," she said, jabbing her finger in the direction of where they'd been. "Surely you don't consider what just happened there a lesson."

"You didn't specify how long these lessons had to last. I feel I've taught you something. Practice holding your sword. And speak to your father. You told me you know the basics. Your instructors have either been inadequate or you lack the ability to grasp basic concepts."

"L-Lack the ability?" she sputtered, so outraged she could barely speak. Oh, how she wanted to plant her fist against his arrogant jaw. It was the first time in her life she ever wanted to strike a man—anyone, actually. "I do not lack ability!"

"Really," he said blandly.

"Yes! *Really*. You hit my sword—" Abruptly, she arrested her words.

"Too hard?" he supplied.

She cringed, embarrassed that he'd guess what she was mistakenly going to say. Her palm and her pride both hurt. She'd never come up against an opponent as large and as strong as Tristan.

"Madame, I assumed you were interested in being able to take on any opponent. Are you only going to fight *women?*" She hated the slight taunt in his tone.

"I *can* fight any opponent. I have only fought men. And I've bested them all!" She stalked away, so scorching was her fury, she wondered if her eyebrows had been singed off. She was infuriated with herself for being so easily beat, and with him for being so insufferable. She didn't care that she was showing too much emotion—knowing full well that by showing anger she was showing weakness—alerting Tristan to the fact that he had enough influence over her to affect her this strongly.

Nor did she care a whit that she was doing what others didn't dare—chastising the mighty Tristan de Tiersonnier.

He needed a dressing-down. He deserved one.

She turned and marched right back up to him again. "You—" She poked him in the chest with her finger. "You are . . . rude! And *arrogant*."

She marched away, picked up her sword, and sheathed it with an angry stab.

Tristan was having a difficult time holding back his smile, the corners of his mouth tugging hard. Her cheeks were pink, her eyes ablaze, and her breasts rose and fell with her quickened breaths. She looked adorable and incredibly alluring in her fiery state.

She stomped back to him. Back for another round. This time Tristan had to fight even harder to keep a straight face.

"And another thing—you know nothing about me." She rose onto the balls of her feet and stuck her pretty face in his. "NOTHING!" She stormed off. Tristan watched her stalk away.

Now, that's not true. He knew she had the sweetest derrière he'd ever seen. In her breeches, it was perfectly defined and inspired an assortment of salacious thoughts. He wanted nothing more than to strip away her clothing, push her down on all fours, grip that luscious behind, and sink his stiff cock into her warm wet core.

She disappeared into the château. At last he allowed himself to break into a smile. *Dieu.* The woman wasn't dull, and she had more fire in her than he'd have guessed. He'd rather direct all that fire into more carnal endeavors.

She is also highly intelligent . . . She couldn't have maintained her elevated status with her father otherwise. Too many royal siblings had tried to knock her off her privileged perch. Without success.

She was crafty. Cunning. And he'd just provoked her in the worst way.

His smile died.

*****

Fool. Fool. Fool! Elisabeth walked across the Grand Salon, making her way to her rooms. Never in her life had she lost her temper like that. Never had she behaved in such an infantile manner.

She'd completely lost control and made a spectacle of herself in front of Tristan. She was mortified. Why did it have to matter how he perceived her? Why couldn't she be indifferent to him the way she was to every other man she'd ever known?

Why would her heart and body not relinquish their incessant longing for this impossible man? For this impossible situation.

You know why, Elisabeth. Besides his masculine beauty, his sexual allure, he was a man with honor. Something rare in her world. Something that touched her deeply. How could she not want him? Despite his personal feelings, he'd stand in front of an assassin's blade for her or anyone else he'd sworn to protect— just as he'd done for the King. That was something she didn't believe the new Captain of the Guard, Antoine de Balzac, would do—and that was yet another reason to see Tristan reinstated.

He was the right man to hold the esteemed position. He deserved it above all others.

"Madame?" Tristan's voice arrested her steps.

By the time she turned, he'd reached her and grabbed hold of her arm. Her in tow, with his cane and his purposeful strides, he ate up the distance to the first door on the right.

Tristan opened it, pulled her inside and slammed the door shut.

She didn't know what to make of his actions or of him pulling off his baldric and tossing it down on the nearby settee. Stupefied, she let him pull hers off as well, without question or protest, and watched as it landed on top of his. His cane followed.

Before she could form a question, he shoved her back against the wall.

Her eyes widened.

Pressing his palm against the wall near her head, he slipped the fingers of his other hand beneath her chin. Her nerve endings sparked to life.

"Why are you here?" he asked.

"You brought me in here." Tingles rippled from his touch down to the tips of her breasts, tightening her nipples.

"I mean at my château. Why have you come here?"

"I told you, I want fencing lessons—"

"That is a lie and we both know it. I want the truth. I want you to admit you're here for your amusement and that you've been purposely behaving like a coquette."

She pushed his fingers away from her chin. It was too difficult to talk when he touched her. "I'm not here for my amusement, and I have not been behaving like a coquette."

He pressed his other palm to the wall, hemming her in between both hands. "No? What do you call this outrageous outfit of yours?"

"My fencing attire. You don't expect me to fence in a gown, do you?" she countered.

"I would expect you to dress like a woman once in a while— and for God's sake, where did you get those boots?"

"What is the matter with my boots? I happen to like them. They're comfortable. As for dressing like a woman, I do. In fact, I did. At supper last eve. You wouldn't know that because you weren't there."

He tilted his head to one side. "Disappointed, were you?"

Oh, she wasn't about to respond to that.

He continued. "Were you saddened you missed out on an opportunity to flirt? To stand too close, and bat your pretty eyes at me?"

Again, she held her tongue and simply gazed up at him, refusing to admit to a thing. It was one thing to attempt to seduce him, quite another to confess to it.

"I am not like those men at court you toy with. If you make sexual overtures to me, you'd better be prepared to be taken and fucked—any way I choose."

Her knees almost gave way. Dear God, how she wished he would fuck her.

He grasped her hand and pressed it to the sizable bulge in his breeches. "This is what you want, what you're trying to accomplish with your teasing, isn't it? To stiffen my cock."

Her sex answered with a warm gush. Through the cloth of his breeches, he felt hard as iron, his proportions more generous in size than any man she'd ever known.

"There aren't going to be any more 'lessons,' any more games. And no more cock-teasing. If you're still here tomorrow night, Duchesse, I am going to fuck you."

Her clit gave a fierce throb, then pulsed in rhythm with her wild heart.

He grasped her wrists, raised them above her head, pinning them against the wall with one hand. Her heart lurched. She tested his hold. His grip was strong and firm. Unbreakable.

"Tristan?" she questioned, his name tumbling from her lips between rapid breaths.

The corner of his mouth rose in a half-smile. "For the first time in your life, you won't be dictating, demanding, or commanding a thing. Tied and bound for my pleasure, you'll submit and surrender your control to me. That's how I'm going to take you. That's how it's going to be."

A jolt of fear rocked her. She wanted to be with him so fiercely . . . but tied and bound? She wasn't afraid he'd harm her in any way, but . . . *surrender her control?* He couldn't possibly be serious. "You—You jest." What was even more frightening was how appealing she found his wicked words. The thought of completely acquiescing to him, not being able to hold back in any way, set her ablaze.

He cupped her breast and pinched her hardened nipple through her shirt. She jerked with a sharp gasp. "No jest. There won't be a part of your body I won't avail myself of." His thumb languidly stroked her nipple, sending delicious sensations swirling down her spine. "You'll be all mine to do with whatever I wish." He pinched her sensitized nipple again. She barely caught her cry of pleasure in time and swallowed it back down. Oh, God. He was serious.

This was no jest.

If she wanted him to take her, it would have to be his way. If she stayed, she'd have to cede to him in the manner he described. He wasn't going to let her finesse her way around it.

Warnings against giving a man complete power over her—especially this man who wielded so much power over her already—sounded in her head.

Ever so lightly he brushed his mouth against her lips. "You'll be at my mercy, Duchesse, and you're going to come harder than you've ever come before."

*****

Tristan rested his head against the back of the chair in the library the next day and swirled the brandy in his goblet.

She'd bolted.

Thirty Musketeers, two carriages, close to forty horses, and two royal daughters—gone.

He'd done it. He'd chased Elisabeth de Roussel away. So why didn't he feel any joy from his accomplishment? Not only had he rid himself of the King's most errant daughter, he'd also gotten rid of the men who'd escorted her. He'd never hidden from anyone or anything in his life, yet he found himself avoiding his former men. The last thing he wanted was for them to watch him moving about in his depleted state. It was more than his pride could bear.

He should be rejoicing at the sudden solitude, but instead he was gripped by the most irritating sense of disappointment.

He wanted Elisabeth. He wanted to do to her everything he'd described. Beneath her masculine clothing was a highly excitable, very feminine form, his every instinct telling him that fucking her would be one of the most intense carnal encounters he'd ever have. He'd seen the arousal in her eyes as well as the fear. She'd been torn between wanting to be possessed and wanting to run.

It had taken all that he had not to taste her and stroke her into an eager willingness, driving everything from her mind except her desire for him. He had to remind himself over and over as his cock throbbed harder than his leg that she wasn't just the daughter of the King, but the daughter whom His Majesty doted upon.

Held most dear.

And, therefore, that made her untouchable as far as he was concerned.

Besides, after Veronique, the last thing he should want was to bed another of the King's daughters. The hot rooms hadn't driven Elisabeth away, nor had the ridiculous "lesson" in fencing he'd given her.

He'd run her off with the promise of a simple sex game, and he wasn't going to waste another moment feeling regret over it.

"Good riddance, Duchesse."

Tristan tipped the goblet and let the brandy flow down his throat, hoping that the burning liquid would take the edge off the pain in his leg.

Fast, hard footsteps approached the library.

His uncle entered the room. "Tristan, are you expecting guests?"

"Guests? No."

"Well, there are a number of men here."

Tristan sat up. "Dear God. Not more Musketeers?"

"No. More like workers."

"What are you taking about?"

Gabriel walked in. "He's talking about the fifty men who are here, clearing the gardens, repairing the façade of the château."

"Fifty men?" Tristan grabbed his cane and struggled to his feet. "Where did they come from?"

Gabriel and Richard exchanged looks.

"You tell him," Gabriel suggested.

"No, I'd rather you be the bearer of bad news."

Tristan didn't like where this was going. "Will someone tell me what is going on?"

Gabriel cleared his throat. "Very well. The workers are here at the behest of the Duchesse de Roussel."

"What?" He couldn't have heard correctly.

"There's more," Richard advised, then turned to Gabriel. "Go on, tell him."

"I'm trying to do that. But I keep getting inter—"

"Get on with it!" Tristan's ire was beginning to mount; he sensed he wasn't going to like what he was about to hear.

Gabriel gave a nod. "Since you are in such a fine mood, I can't wait to tell you the rest." His sarcasm only served to grate on Tristan's taunt nerves. "We were a tad mistaken when we told you earlier that the Duchesse de Roussel had left."

Tristan's stomach clenched. *"Merde.* You jest."

"No. I don't. It turns out, she took it upon herself to change rooms," Gabriel continued. "You see when we saw that the Musketeers and the trunks were gone, we assumed the Duchesse and her sister had left—permanently. We were unaware that their trunks were moved to the west wing."

"The west wing? Where my . . . *our* rooms are?"

Gabriel sauntered over to him and placed a hand on Tristan's shoulder. "Precisely."

Tristan tightened his jaw. "Where is the Duchesse now?"

His brother shrugged. "Who knows? She's out and about with her entourage. In the meantime, we are having some lovely repairs done to our château." He smiled.

By the looks on his uncle's and brother's faces, they were pleased.

Tristan was ready to strangle the King's favorite child. The woman was beyond intrusive. She knew no boundaries.

The sound of horses' hooves striking the cobblestones in the courtyard grabbed his attention. He rushed out of the library and down the tapestry-lined hall.

The moment Tristan entered the vestibule, he froze. So did his breathing.

Standing on the opposite side of the grand entrance, talking to her sister and her maid, Elisabeth was in a yellow gown embellished with golden bows. Her tantalizing form was outlined so enticingly, his mouth went dry.

As though she felt his gaze, she turned and smiled when she saw him. Immediately, she approached. Her dark hair adorned with small golden bows was perfectly coiffed, long silky curls he wanted to touch. His hungry gaze devoured her, moving down to her décolletage, enjoying the sweet little bounce of her breasts with each step she took.

Her bedazzling smile was still on her lovely face when she reached him. She looked like an angel.

She folded her hands before her. "Good day, gentlemen."

He peeled his eyes off her and looked beside him. *Dieu*, he'd been so transfixed, he hadn't even realized his brother and uncle flanked him.

They exchanged pleasantries, while Tristan, for the first time in his life, was speechless.

"I hope you don't mind that I left for a bit of an outing," she said to him. "I purchased something for you in the town." She motioned to her maid and sister.

The moment the maid handed Elisabeth the wooden box she carried, Claire gave a giggle then quickly looked down, covering her mouth with her fingertips.

Elisabeth handed him the box and opened the lid for him. Filling the box were numerous silk scarves.

"They're for later," Elisabeth said.

His gaze shot up to hers. She was smiling still and with a wink, sauntered away, heading toward the staircase that led to the west wing. Another giggle erupted from Claire before she quickly fell in step with her sister and servant.

Jésus-Christ. The scarves were for binding—her. He hadn't scared her away. She'd called his bluff.

She meant to *stay*.

Gabriel sifted his hand through the scarves and frowned. "These are for women. *Merde*, brother, she dresses like a man. If you're going to start dressing like a woman, I don't wish to know about it."

Tristan gnashed his teeth. The noise outside, from the workers, the newly returned Musketeers, and their horses, all merged into a nerve-grating clamor invading the inner sanctum of his home. The hammering outside was keeping time with the throbbing in his cock. Once again he was stiff as steel. Once again his château was overrun.

All because of the most ungovernable woman he'd ever met.

Tristan slammed the box shut, tucked it under his arm, and limped toward the staircase with the aid of his cane.

Most unwise to give a man who wishes to strangle an unruly woman the very means by which to do it.

CHAPTER FOUR

"Do you think Tristan will be here soon?" Claire asked while seated comfortably in Elisabeth's newly acquired rooms. The private apartments on the west side of the château were not only cooler, but better furnished and far more pleasant.

"I predict within the next few minutes." Elisabeth voice sounded calm, giving no indication of just how discomposed she was. She stood near the windows, too nervous to sit, her stomach in knots. She'd just made a bold move downstairs. The boldest in her life.

The next step was up to Tristan.

He was angry at her—for reasons she fully expected him to voice when he entered her rooms—but he was also undeniably interested in following through with his vow. She'd seen arousal flare in his eyes when he saw the contents of the wooden box.

Her very entrails quaked with anticipation. An amorous encounter was at hand. With tall, strong, beautiful Tristan de Tiersonnier. The notion made her feel warm, weak, and a bit apprehensive—especially when she thought about how he was going to take her.

She'd never done anything like this in her life.

Claire burst into a giggle. Elisabeth jumped a little. Claire's spontaneous fits of joviality hadn't ceased since Elisabeth purchased the scarves and told her of their intended purpose.

"Did you see the look on Tristan's face when you handed him the box of scarves? I can't believe you're going to let him do something so wicked," Claire said.

Neither could she. His provocative promise consumed her every waking thought and had teased and tantalized her all last night. She'd vacillated, and in the end, she decided she'd come too far to quit now. She was so very close to having him. It was what she'd come there for.

It was the only way to douse the fire.

The door to her antechamber swung open.

Tristan entered, a scowl on his handsome face, the wooden box under his arm. He dropped the box onto the marble top table in the room with a clunk.

A fresh wave of nervous excitement crested over her. "A knock before entering a lady's apartments is customary, is it not, Tristan?" Elisabeth said.

His nostrils flared. "I'll do as I bloody well please. This is my home. A concept you don't seem to grasp." He spoke in a low snarl, slowly advancing upon her, his purpose to intimidate, no doubt. She rooted her feet to the floor to keep from bolting from the room. "You don't change rooms at will. You don't order my staff to move your trunks about. And you certainly do not hire men to alter my château! Do you understand?" he barked, stopping before her.

Clearly, he was quite livid. Perhaps the workers were too much to add to the mix today.

"Yes, Tristan. Of course." Her mother had taught her that the best way to counter a man's ire was with soft tones. Agreeable words. If she had anything at stake, a woman only stood to lose, to suffer, if she didn't promptly calm the storm.

Elisabeth had something at stake. He wouldn't take her when he was this angry.

Yet unlike her dealings with other men, she didn't want to simply voice empty words just to appease him. For the first time ever, Elisabeth found herself wanting to offer a man an explanation. It actually mattered to her that she made him understand.

"Claire." Her sister had shot to her feet the moment Tristan had barged into the room. Warily, Claire watched the exchange between Elisabeth and Tristan. "Why don't you go back to your rooms. I shall speak to you later," Elisabeth said.

Claire glanced at Tristan and then back at her. "Ar-Are you certain?"

"Quite certain," she assured her with a smile.

Reluctantly, her sister murmured a "good day" and left Elisabeth's new apartments.

Elisabeth tried to ignore the wild fluttering in her stomach. She was, for the first time, alone with Tristan in her chambers. She folded her hands before her. Just being this close to him made her quiver. "Now then, I seem to have angered you. That wasn't my intent. The men were hired as a gesture of thanks."

"Thanks? For what?"

"For two reasons: first, for my personal gratitude for your years of loyal service to the King and our family."

She saw the surprise in his eyes. An expression she couldn't name crossed his face, and his features softened slightly. Her words had come from her heart. His effect on her was so strong, she had to be careful not to go any further. Not to offer up any more emotional revelations.

"The second reason for the workers was in thanks for the fencing lessons. On the day we arrived, I sent one of the men to you with a sizable purse as payment—though at the time I didn't know your lessons would be quite so brief. In any event, you wouldn't accept payment. That night I had two of His Majesty's Guard ride back to Versailles with the order to return with gardeners and workers. What I did was meant as a gift. I had hoped you'd be pleased. Obviously, I misjudged your reaction." All right, perhaps that wasn't the *whole* truth. She'd hoped to fix up the château lest the King see it in its current state. It would help cast a more favorable light on Tristan as a potential husband. "The men will cease immediately, if that's what you wish. As to the changing of the rooms, you and I both know you purposely placed me in rooms that were uncomfortable. You want me gone. Clearly, I've earned your disdain."

He remained silent. His expression was guarded.

Elisabeth pressed on, her heart pounding. "It is because you think I'm spoiled. His Majesty's favorite daughter, privileged and self-indulgent. Oh, and yes, let us not forget a *coquette*. That accurately sums it up, doesn't it?"

He took a deep breath and let it out slowly. In a softer voice than before, he said, "Actually, it does, madame." The man believed in being honest—even when that honesty had bite. Still, it made him a better man than others she knew. She didn't know any other honest men.

"Tell me, Tristan, how many men have you seen around me at court?"

"Many," he said without hesitation.

"And of those men, how many have you seen me turn away?"

"Almost all."

"And did it ever occur to you that I may have had good reason to reject them?"

"Really," he said dryly. "What reason would you have?"

"Because I know they wanted to bed me simply to get close to the King."

He cocked a brow.

"The King's favorite daughter has great appeal to those driven by ambition, Tristan. You've been at court. You've seen the maneuvering. The backstabbing. Too many of the men have no qualms about using a woman to get to the King. I refuse to be used that way." She never left herself open to it. By maintaining an emotional distance, a level of detachment, she was able to keep a proper prospective and see the scheming. She never fell for false words of affection and devotion. Her mother had taught her that a woman had to be strong, stay strong, and never—not ever—allow herself to be vulnerable in matters of the heart. It clouded a woman's judgment. Should Tristan become her husband, she still had to distance herself emotionally. Even as his wife, she couldn't permit herself to continue to feel the things she felt for him.

It laid her bare. And a woman could never do that.

Too many women had made the mistake of allowing tender sentiment to go unchecked for their husbands or lovers—to their detriment. At times, to their ruin.

With Tristan, she'd already broken too many of the rules she lived by.

"I'm selective, Tristan. Not coquettish. There is a difference. Besides my husband, I've only been with two men." She'd never admit she'd given herself to Selle and Leymont with the hopes of quashing her yearning for Tristan.

Unfortunately, it hadn't worked.

He gave a nod. "The Marquis de Leymont and the Duc de Selle."

He'd noticed? He'd watched her that closely? *Of course he had. It was his duty. He was responsible for the welfare of the royal family.* He was supposed to know who was in the inner circle.

Elisabeth looked down at her hands and immediately squelched her disappointment.

"Everyone thinks that being the favorite daughter of the King is an enviable position to be in." She looked up at him. "It has its serious flaws. The King gave his favorite daughter to his friend, the Duc de Roussel, as a gesture of his esteem for the man. It didn't matter that the Duc was twenty-five years my senior. That he had no interest in having another wife, or any more children. The Duc accepted his "gift." Shortly after our marriage, Roussel shipped me to his country château. I lived in that dilapidated drafty abode for three years—until the Duc's death—so I am not as pampered as you think."

He studied her quietly for a moment. "This is the first time I've ever heard you be in any way candid. It is a pleasant surprise."

It was true. It was the first time she'd been this candid with anyone. As wrong as she knew it was, it felt good to open herself up a little to him.

He reached out, grasped her arm, and pulled her to him. She collided against his hard body. A jolt of sensations shot through her distended nipples the moment they came in contact with his chest. She barely caught her moan in time.

He snaked his arm around her waist, that impressive part of his male anatomy pressing so tantalizingly against her belly. "Why have you come to me? I want the truth."

"I want lessons from the finest swordsman in the land," she said honestly, having always been in awe of his skill.

He removed his arm from around her waist and placed a warm hand at the nape of her neck. "Why else?" Again his voice was soft and it set her belly aflutter.

Gazing up into his beautiful blue eyes, she silently begged him to kiss her, needing it with jarring desperation, the bud between her legs pulsating wildly, each hungry throb a torment. *Say it, Elisabeth. It's just three words. Tell him the truth here, or this won't happen.*

"I . . . want you." She'd never said that to any man and meant it.

"You're truly going to let me have you?"

"Yes."

"I warn you, Duchesse, once we begin, I'm not going to stop, so if you're having any qualms . . ."

She shook her head. "No qualms. I won't stop you."

The most sensual smile lifted the corner of his mouth. "Excellent. Then you're mine." He lowered his head.

She held her breath and braced herself for the thrill of his lips. He didn't disappoint. At the first touch of his mouth, he sent a hot rush streaming through her body, leaving her toes tingling. He tasted better than any man had a right to. Better than she'd dreamed. His tongue pushed past her quivering lips and possessed her mouth with a hot thrust. Her sex tightened in response and in anticipation of his possession yet to come, of his cock in her core.

His hand held her head securely, and he angled it slightly, confidently commanding her senses the way only a master of the carnal arts could. She gripped his strong shoulders and held on in the maelstrom of sensations radiating out from the feel of his body pressed so sumptuously against hers, and his heated, hungry kiss.

His mouth was gone.

She snapped her eyes open, bereft, dazed. Ravenous.

He was watching her. "I like the way you taste." His voice was darkly sensuous. Removing his hand from the nape of her neck, he lightly trailed the pads of his fingers over the tops of her breasts. Her breathing hitched. "How wet are you for me?"

She had to swallow first. "Very."

"Good. I can't wait to taste you everywhere, especially your sweet sex." She didn't know how much more of this her body could take. She was ready to shatter into orgasm on the spot.

"Are you ready to be bound and taken?" he asked. Her knees weakened.

Oh, God. He was so sinfully delicious. This was beyond any fantasy she'd had of him. Far more carnal than she'd ever imagined. Her sex wept.

Dipping his head, he said in her ear, "Tell me you want it. Tell me you want to be bound and taken."

Out of her mouth—the mouth of a woman who was always tightly guarded—tumbled, "Yes! Yes, I want it."

He pulled back and gazed down at her. She could tell by the smile in his eyes that her answer pleased him. "Tell me what it's doing to you to know I'm about to tie you with the scarves you so graciously provided and feed your cunt my cock."

She shivered and fisted his shirt. "I . . . can't." She didn't know how to put voice to it. This man was too overpowering for her senses. He always had her off balance. He was pushing her beyond her limits.

Tristan carefully gauged her reactions. She trembled, her breathing quick, and her skin was flushed from her cheeks to the tops of her breasts. *Dieu*, she was so responsive. With so little effort, he could undo her.

He liked that.

What he didn't like was the nervousness he detected. He didn't want her to be nervous or tense.

"Have you ever played sex games before, Elisabeth? Have you ever had a man bind your wrists and legs apart?"

"No," she said softly.

This was going to be a first for her. The thought quickened his heart.

"I want you to relax and enjoy the experience. I won't do anything you don't wish me to do. You have my word."

Her large hazel eyes held his firmly. "I know. I trust you," she said without hesitation. That this strong, spirited, beautiful woman was bestowing such trust in him by allowing him to bind her moved him. Layers were being peeled away, and he was seeing sides of Elisabeth he'd never seen before.

Sides of her he liked. Very much.

She stepped away from him, retrieved the wooden box with the scarves, and handed it to him. "Take me."

Sweeter words were never spoken from sweeter lips. He'd heard those very words from other women, but when she said them, it rocked him, his thick cock jerking hard and hungrily.

"Sweet Elisabeth, I am going to take you in ways you've never been taken before. And you're going to enjoy every one of them." He gestured toward the bedchamber. "After you, my lady."

Entering the bedchamber with Elisabeth, Tristan spilled the contents of the box on the bed and tossed the box and his cane aside. It occurred to him that for the first time since his injury, his leg was hardly bothering him.

Impatient, he turned to Elisabeth, hauled her up against him and claimed her mouth. She moaned softly and immediately laced her arms around his neck, her body molding so perfectly to his. She felt wonderful in his arms. His tongue invaded her mouth, plundering the soft recesses, enjoying the way she returned his kisses with equal hunger. There were so many reasons he should stop. So many reasons not to take her. But as he stripped away her clothing, revealing her soft skin a little more with each article he removed, those reasons fell away with her attire. He couldn't come up with an argument strong enough to make him push her away. Not when he wanted her this much. Not when his sac was so heavy and so tight. Not when his prick pounded in rhythm with his wild heart.

Her eager hands opened his breeches. Tristan yanked his shirt off, tossed it away and sat down on the edge of the bed.

Standing before him in her knee-length chemise and *caleçons*, Elisabeth's gaze was riveted to his erect cock boldly protruding from his breeches. She bit her lip, her confidence faltering briefly. He hid his smile.

"We're going to be the perfect fit," he assured her. He knew he was big, but he also knew how to use every inch of his length and girth to pleasure a woman.

He removed the last articles of clothing from her body, then paused to admire the beauty before him. Lush curves, gorgeous breasts with the pinkest most mouthwatering nipples he'd ever seen. At mouth level to him, they were erect and begging to be touched, sucked.

"You are beautiful," he murmured and pulled her closer. Her hands gripped his shoulders and he felt her tense, bracing for his touch. She thought he was going to go straight to the sensitive tips that were pebbled and straining for him. Instead, he ran his hands slowly, teasingly around the contours of her perfect tits, purposely avoiding the taut peaks. Her fingers dug into his arms. She closed her eyes and arched to him—her silent demand for more. Watching for her reaction, he lightly brushed his fingertips across her nipples. She gave a soft cry and shuddered.

He smiled.

Grasping her hips, Tristan leaned in and kissed around each nipple, building her excitement, her anticipation for when he finally suckled her.

She jerked and tried to press her nipple to his mouth.

Tristan pulled away, smiling. "No, you don't, *chérie*. I'll get there when I get there."

"I . . . can't take any more."

Despite the urgency thundering inside him, he was intent on savoring her. "Yes, you can." Then he licked the underside of her breast. She made a strangled sound.

Tristan turned her around, her pert bottom now facing him. "Give me your wrists."

Shaking, Elisabeth put her hands behind her back for him. "Do it. *Hurry.*" She'd never been so lost to sexual abandon. Never had she been on fire like this. Gripped by carnal cravings, her nervousness had disappeared.

Grabbing one of the scarves off the bed, he bound her wrists together, then spun her back around. His hot mouth immediately latched onto her breast, sucking her nipple in. She cried out, her knees all but buckling beneath her. She might have fallen to the floor if it hadn't been for his strong arm around her waist, holding her. He sucked her other nipple and moved back to the first, his teeth and hot tongue creating sensations that reverberated in her sheath, her feminine muscles tightening and releasing of their own accord.

He was most definitely not hurrying.

Clearly, he was intent on torturing her with his inflaming mouth in the most exquisite way.

Securely in his hold, her wrists bound behind her back, she couldn't do anything other than drown in the pleasure flooding her body. Her head fell back and she squeezed her eyes shut, rapid breaths dragging in and out of her lungs.

His tongue gave her nipple a final flick.

"On your belly, Elisabeth." He rose, thankfully keeping a firm hold on her waist; she wasn't certain her legs would support her weight. "Keep your feet on the floor." Moving her to the edge of the bed, he bent her forward, and lowered her torso down onto the mattress.

The coolness of the counterpane against the overheated skin on her breasts and her belly made her gasp. Looking over her shoulder, she saw him strip away the remainder of his clothing, her eyes drinking in his perfect physique, all muscular and sinewy, and his impressive cock. Arousal quavered in her belly. He moved behind her and skimmed his hands down her arms to her bound wrists.

"Are your arms all right?" he asked, setting his palms on her bare bottom. She wiggled, her skin feeling extra sensitive. Unable to summon her voice, she simply nodded. Tristan caressed her derrière. "You've been driving me out of my fucking mind in those breeches of yours. They show off this fine part of your anatomy. I couldn't resist having you this way."

Dear God, couldn't he just get on with it?

"Spread your legs for me," he ordered.

At last! Quickly, she complied, widening her stance. The cool air against her wet private flesh made her shiver.

He lowered himself down onto his knee, her sex open for his viewing. A smooth scarf was suddenly around one ankle, his hands quickly binding it to the bedpost, repeating the same action with her other ankle, securing her legs apart.

His strong masculine hands skimmed up her legs. "*Christ*, you're the most arousing sight I've ever seen." He cupped her slick sex with a warm palm. She gasped and lurched but couldn't move far. "So wet for me." Tristan rubbed her lightly, a gentle stroking of his hand over her sensitive flesh, not enough to make her come, just enough to keep her keen. Hungry. Tormented.

He leaned a little closer. "You look delicious and ready for any way I want to claim this pretty sex." His warm breath tickled against her bottom. She felt him part her folds, and then came the slow swipe of his tongue. She jerked and whimpered, the bud between her legs aching for his attention. He licked around it, and she suspected he was avoiding her clit on purpose, knowing she was wavering on the edge of a stunning release. Bound as she was, she was unable to press hard against his mouth the way she longed to. She was at the mercy of his mouth, his every wicked lick over her erogenous flesh.

He slid his hot tongue inside her. She curled her toes, the sound of pleasure bursting from her lips.

"The sweetest cream," he groaned. "I could make you come with my mouth, but I'm going to do it with my cock instead." She heard him stand.

Before she could rejoice, his fingers slid inside her. She didn't know how many fingers, but knew he was using enough to create a delicious pressure, his skillful hand lightly pumping her, making her moan.

"You're so tight. How do you want it, Elisabeth? Slow and deep? Hard and fast?"

She tightened around his fingers, desperate and so out of control. So out of character. On unfamiliar ground. "I want it this minute. Right now!" No man had ever touched her the way he did.

He chuckled, leaned over her and kissed her shoulder. "I see you've found your voice," he said in her ear and then straightened, pulled his fingers out of her and gripped her hips.

"How's this?" He butted the head of his shaft at the slit of her sex. A sound shot up her throat, a mixture of a moan and a sob of joy. Tristan pressed forward, his cock stretching her as he fed it to her one slow inch at a time. She couldn't hold back the sultry sounds she made. He was so large. This moment monumental. A fantasy come true. A dream brought to life.

And she was afraid.

It was suddenly too much. He was too much for her. The moment too intense. Would she be the same afterward—after she completely abandoned herself to him?

He swore. "Relax. Don't tense. Take me in . . ."

You want this. You ache for him! You've got to have him. Taking a deep breath, she released the tension in her body. He felt it immediately and drove his cock into her deeper than any man had ever been.

Elisabeth cried out, so completely filled and possessed.

"Oh, yes," he groaned, filling her again and again, driving away any sense of emptiness. Quickly, he picked up the pace and she reveled in it. "You feel *incredible*."

He rode her, hard and fast, his grip on her hips tight, his sizable sex creating stunning sensations, the likes of which she'd never known.

Her helpless body took every fierce thrust, rejoicing in each one as he plunged and dragged his solid shaft.

Elisabeth dug her nails into her palms, unable to control the contractions quivering through her sheath. She sagged heavily on the bed. Her legs were shaking so badly, they were no longer capable of holding any of her weight. Yet she arched, lifting her bottom high, straining toward him to take him in as deeply as she could.

Her release was imminent. She buried her face in the counterpane, not wanting to let go. Not wanting this perfect pleasure to end.

His powerful thrusts were gloriously unrelenting, driving her closer to the edge. "Come for me. I can feel how close you are, clenching and pulsing around me."

She was. She couldn't stop it. She couldn't stop the orgasm thundering down on her.

A large hot wave slammed into her, vaulting her into ecstasy. She screamed into the mattress, rapture flooding her body. He drove in harder, ramming her repeatedly as Elisabeth basked in the sublime sensations, her sex wildly pulsating around him with each spasm of her slick walls.

Tristan suddenly reared. His palms came down hard on the mattress near her shoulders and he gave a long, deep groan, his warm semen shooting onto her back.

Elisabeth pressed her cheek against the counterpane and briefly closed her eyes, the contractions of vaginal muscles ebbing, her heart and breathing slowly returning to normal.

Tristan lightly bit her shoulder. She flinched, turned her head, and found herself gazing into his sensual blue eyes. He was smiling, looking so beautiful, it made her stomach flutter. He kissed the spot on her shoulder where he'd bitten her, then straightened, untied her hands and ankles, and wiped her clean with a scarf.

Elisabeth didn't move. Her muscles were so lax, she didn't think she could. He picked her up as if she weighed nothing at all and deposited her in the middle of the bed. Stretching out beside her, he propped himself onto his elbow and began to knead one of her wrists.

"Are you all right? Are your arms sore?"

She'd never felt better. She'd never felt this kind of bliss in her life. "I'm fine."

His smile broadened. "That was very good." Closer to incredible, she wanted to say. In fact, it was beautiful and intense, just like the man beside her. "There is definitely a delicious carnal connection between us."

She couldn't argue with that. The fire between them burned white-hot.

He tilted her chin up and gave her a long inebriating kiss. "Now that we've taken the edge off, I can fuck you slowly the rest of the night . . . and into the morning."

Into the morning? He meant to stay the night? *No, you should ask him to leave once you're done.* She never allowed men to stay after sex. Neither Selle nor Leymont was permitted to remain. And as for her late husband, he'd thankfully left promptly after their brief one-time copulation. Having consummated the marriage, he departed for his hôtel in Paris and never touched her again.

The thought of spending the night with Tristan had her body vibrating with renewed hunger. It was astounding that he could inflame her so quickly, so easily, after such a strong orgasm, with just his words. That alone was a good enough reason to refuse and put a bit of distance between them.

But instead, she told herself it was a better idea to stay with him through the night. She told herself that this was part of her plan; she was, after all, trying to have her fill of this man.

Then she wrapped her arms around him, snuggled close to his hard body, and gazed into his stirring eyes.

"I'd love that, Tristan."

She told herself she had the situation well in hand.

Chapter Five

His cock was in heaven. As Tristan drifted out of sleep and into consciousness, the glorious sensations swamping his shaft became stronger, the wet heat enveloping it—keener, and the soft sucking noises in the quiet room—louder.

He opened his eyes, looked down his body, and was met with the erotic sight of Elisabeth drawing on his hard prick, her head lowering and rising in a steady, sublime rhythm. He closed his eyes briefly and smiled.

Is there a better way to greet the morning than waking up to a beautiful woman sucking you off?

Last night had been delicious. Today was starting out just as fine.

She gently cupped his sac, and he groaned. She looked up, his cock popping out of her mouth when she met his gaze.

Her smile was radiant, her cheeks slightly flushed. "Good morning." She sat back on her heels, yet still held on to the base of his shaft. Rays from the morning sun shone into the room, allowing him the pleasure of seeing her lovely naked form in the bright light of the day.

"Good morning, Elisabeth." Images of her bound by silk scarves, wet and eager, filled his mind. Memories he'd never forget. Last eve wasn't the first time he'd engaged in that kind of sex play, but with Elisabeth, it had been different. She was different from any woman he'd had.

She was different from the woman he'd believed her to be.

And she made him feel different than he'd been feeling the last three months.

Since his injury, he'd felt depleted and diminished. It didn't escape his notice that not once since her arrival had Elisabeth treated him as anything but whole. Not like a man with an infirmity. She'd treated him simply as a man—fully capable. And had even demanded fencing lessons. Lessons he intended to provide her with—proper lessons this time.

"I hope you don't mind," she said, leisurely stroking his cock from base to tip in her warm fist, his greedy prick luxuriating in the pleasure radiating along its length. "But I noticed this particular part of your anatomy—of impressive proportions, I might add—was awake and looking for attention."

She drew another smile from him. She was the only one who'd made him smile since his injury. "I don't mind at all," he said. "By all means, help yourself."

Mischief twinkled in her eyes. "Thank you, sir. I must admit I find you rather delicious."

He chuckled, but his laugh was choked off by a gasp the moment she lowered her head and gave the tip of his cock a lush lick.

Elisabeth plunged him deep into her mouth. He closed his eyes and hissed out the air from his lungs. Intent on delving his fingers into her soft dark hair and guiding her movements, he reached for her, only to have his hands stopped short.

What in the world . . . ? He snapped open his eyes and looked up. His wrists were bound with silk scarves to the outside posts of the bed.

He shot a look at Elisabeth.

She drew him from her mouth. "It's just a sex game. I thought I'd return the favor."

He was a leader. Dominant by nature—in and out of the boudoir. "I don't get tied up."

She tilted her head to one side. "Really?" She was doing a poor job of hiding her smile. "I'd say, by the looks of things, you do. Now just relax and enjoy the experience." *Merde*. Those were the very words he'd said to her last night.

"Elisabeth." There was a distinct command in his voice, a sharpness to his tone that always arrested anyone's actions.

Except the woman kneeling between his legs.

Lowering her head, she plunged him back into her hot moist mouth, tearing a groan from his throat, and immediately resumed her rhythmic sucks.

He glanced at one of the posts he was tied to and tested the binding by giving it a yank. To his surprise, the knot gave. As he tried the other knot securing his other arm, it gave, too.

Tristan glanced back at the spirited woman pleasuring him, completely unaware that he could, with moderate effort, free himself.

She pulled his prick from her mouth, and licked her lips. His rock-hard cock pulsed, famished for more. "You know, I don't know what I find more delectable—your taste or having the mighty Tristan de Tiersonnier tied to my bed, at my mercy."

He hid his amusement. She wanted to play games.

Oh, he'd play. His way.

Looking adorably smug, she crawled up his body, her sweet face stopping inches from his. "I can do whatever I want to you," she teased. Her palms were pressed into the mattress on either side of his chest, her knees on either side of his hips. He detected the faint scent of her arousal. She was wet; her little sex play was exciting her.

He looked down and took a moment to admire her pretty breasts. Her nipples were hard, looking like two tempting berries he just had to taste.

"Put one of your nipples in my mouth." To toy with her, he purposely worded the phrase as a command.

A slight frown pulled her delicate brows together. She was clearly dismayed over his lack of submissiveness. "You are in no position to dictate—"

"The left one. I'll start with that."

"I don't think you understand. You're tied up . . ."

Angling his head, he bent his knees, the tops of his thighs bumping her soft bottom, sending her body forward—one tasty teat landing in his ready mouth.

He sucked. She gasped sharply. Tristan snapped the knots binding his wrists, wrapped his arms around her to hold her still, and drove his cock up into her warm dewy sheath. She gave a cry. He groaned. The quick movement had sent a jolt of pain down his leg, but it was a small price to pay in comparison to the pleasure of being back inside her hot tight cunt. He'd had her most of last night, yet he wanted her again with untamed intensity.

"I hope you don't mind," he said. "But I noticed there were parts of your anatomy that were awake and looking for attention." Tristan bit and laved her nipple while giving her long luscious strokes with his shaft, building her slowly and steadily into a frenzy. She shivered, seductive sounds escaping her with each soft pant. He couldn't believe he'd ever thought this woman was a tease. She was sensual, passionate, a woman who enjoyed sex as much as he did. Yet she was more than just a good tumble.

She rocked her hips, trying to dictate the pace, to quicken the tempo, unable to contain the urge. He easily thwarted her efforts, his tight embrace holding her still as he drove in deep with deliberate thrusts. She made a sound at the back of her throat, and slumped slightly against him, her body completely yielding to his possession; all attempts at control had slipped away from her.

Her surrender drove him wild, made him fuck her harder. Faster. Arching to him, she mewed loudly.

He loved fucking her.

He loved having this alluring willful fiery woman completely abandon herself to him.

Though bedding the King's most cherished daughter wasn't the wisest thing he'd ever done, he couldn't seem to muster any regret.

Releasing her wet distended nipple from his mouth, he lightly pinched and rolled it as he turned to her other breast and suckled its sensitive tip.

His name rushed past her lips on a ragged breath. She tightened her juicy walls around his thrusting cock, bathing it with a fresh gush of warm cream. It inflamed him further. His heart hammered. His sac was so tight and full, he could barely hold on to the load of come.

A light sheen of perspiration coated their bodies. Tristan released her nipples and rolled her onto her back, the force of each solid plunge of his prick driving her into the mattress. He claimed her soft mouth in a ravenous kiss, shoving his tongue past her lips. Her arms encircled him, an endearing embrace, and she shuddered.

She was beginning to come. He could tell by the sweet sting of her nails on his back, the pulling of her cunt, and the tensing and arching of her body. He braced himself. Tearing her mouth from his, she threw her head back and screamed in orgasm. Her sex contracted around his cock.

Tristan gripped the sheets in a white-knuckle hold, thrusting, knowing he was about to go over the edge any moment. On the next fierce pull of her sex, he reared, jerking out his cock in the nick of time, sending hot blasts of come onto her belly. He threw his head back and bellowed out his pleasure until the last draining drops poured from his prick.

On all fours, he hung his head, trying to catch his breath, not caring a whit that his leg was punishing him for this position. He looked down at Elisabeth. Her skin was flushed. The nipples he'd feasted on were still hard, but her features were soft, a warm smile adorning her lips. She looked sated. Beautiful.

Jésus-Christ, he could easily get used to this if he wasn't careful.

Theirs was a brief, temporary arrangement. Elisabeth wasn't Veronique. He couldn't keep her as his mistress, and it was certain the King's thoughts had turned to marrying her off again. He'd heard His Majesty's comments with his own ears.

Her next husband was sure to be someone notable, of significant standing. Like the late Duc de Roussel.

She reached out and caressed his cheek. Rising up on her elbows, she kissed him, a soft sensuous meeting of the mouths. "I love what you do to me," she said with touching sincerity.

The problem was, he loved doing it to her—a little too much.

*****

"Elisabeth, did you hear me?"

Claire's voice broke through Elisabeth's thoughts. She dragged her gaze from the window to her sister. Sitting in Elisabeth's apartments, wearing a green brocade gown, her younger sibling was frowning.

"I'm sorry, Claire. What did you say?"

"You said you've devised a plan for tomorrow. What is it?"

"Ah, yes, tomorrow's plan." Elisabeth turned toward the window again, easily locating Tristan among the many men below. Five days of the most indescribable bliss she'd spent with that man. Fencing and making love with Tristan de Tiersonnier. Could there be anything finer? Unable to hold back her smile, Elisabeth watched as he spoke to a group of the King's Guard. Their respect and regard for him were evident on their faces and in their stance even from her second-floor vantage point. There was no doubt about it, Tristan was still the Captain in their hearts. If she had anything to do with it, he was going to be their Captain in truth once more.

"Tomorrow is the day of the King's monthly hunt," Elisabeth said, turning away from the window. "In attendance will be the usual courtiers—who'll be vying for the King's attention—and their wives." Disdain crept into Elisabeth's voice. Having been around powerful men all her life, she should have been accustomed by now to the way they used women. Yet, it still bothered her to see women serve as pawns for social promotion. It happened in so many ways—through marriages, the swapping of mistresses, and in His Majesty's case, well, she couldn't count the number of times she'd seen men subtly and not so subtly offer up their wives to the King just to gain his favor—as dispassionately as one would offer a ride on a horse.

It didn't help that her father had a roving eye and had been known on occasion to express his interest in another man's wife—*sans* the offer. Her own mother had been a married woman when she became his royal mistress.

The more she was with Tristan, the more she hated the artifice that soiled her life. And the artifice she was forced to use just for her and her sister Claire to survive.

"Yes, yes. I know all that," Claire said. "What I don't understand is why you want to leave here to attend? You don't like the hunts. You don't care for those who attend them—and I thought your point for being here was to enjoy Tristan. Why leave before the week's end?"

"Because we are going to get Tristan reinstated as Captain of the Guard."

Claire's brows shot up. "We are? Why?"

"Because I quite enjoy him and wish him to be back at the palace—where I can continue to enjoy him." How she wished that was all there was to it. How she wished there wasn't any emotional longing involved. But her feelings for Tristan had only deepened.

Last night, lying in Tristan's arms as he slept, she'd decided the King's hunt offered an opportunity she couldn't pass up. One whereby Tristan could impress her father. With her affections now stronger, her desire for him keener than ever before, she couldn't simply finish her week with Tristan and let it end there. She decided to cut the time short, gamble, and possibly gain something more permanent.

Thus, the need to escalate her plan.

Claire cocked her head to one side. "Is that the only reason? You're going to have Balzac removed just to have easier access to your lover?" There was something in Claire's eyes that gave Elisabeth unease. A certain knowing look—as though she was seeing inside her heart. *Impossible.* She hadn't become that transparent about her feelings for Tristan.

Had she?

Dismissing the notion as absurd, Elisabeth continued, "No. As a matter of fact, there is another reason. Antoine de Balzac is no better than the rest of the men at court, and well you know it, Claire. He shouldn't be the Captain of the Musketeers if he is corruptible, which he is. And what's equally worrisome is that he and Veronique are now lovers."

Not exactly the primary motivation driving her plan, but it was all she was ready to admit to and far easier to voice than her undying love for Tristan.

Claire frowned and gave a nod. "Veronique only welcomes Balzac into her bed because of his esteemed position. As the commander of the Guard, he is close to the King. She wants to get close to the King through Balzac. She wants to replace you in His Majesty's affections, become his favorite daughter, and reap the benefits that come with it."

Unfortunately, that was true.

Elisabeth had better apartments, better treatment from the courtiers, more influence than her lesser siblings. Veronique wanted to take that from her.

It worried her. In truth, deep down inside it terrified her. With the ruthlessness of Veronique and others at court, if she lost her standing with the King, God only knew what would become of Claire. Or her.

"We cannot let Veronique succeed in her schemes," Elisabeth said. It was all about survival. Those who didn't have the favor of the King were treated poorly and had a miserable existence at the palace.

Elisabeth had Claire to think about. To protect. Even when she was married to the Duc, Elisabeth had protected Claire and had kept her sister with her at the Duc's château, away from the glittering corrupt court of Versailles.

If Veronique ever managed to win favor and any kind of influence with the King, she'd cause undue misery to Elisabeth and Claire, simply because she could. Simply to exercise her power. A power Elisabeth had, but never abused in her privileged position.

Born months apart, Veronique and Elisabeth had always been rivals. Elisabeth's mother had replaced Veronique's mother, Diane, as the King's favorite mistress. Diane had spent the rest of her days trying to gain preferential treatment for her daughter she couldn't get for herself.

Since her mother's recent death, Veronique had not relented in her ambition to advance her status at court. It motivated her every action. Her every move.

Veronique was using the unwitting Balzac in her plot—positioning and angling—trying to get close enough to the King to affect his choice, to influence the King in selecting a powerful husband for her. Elisabeth didn't care who Veronique married, though she suspected Veronique had someone high ranking in mind. If Elisabeth hoped to secure a better match for herself this time around—and a good match for Claire—she couldn't lose her standing.

Once Claire had a good husband, she'd be safe. And Elisabeth could then breathe a sigh of relief. Elisabeth's betrothal to the Duc had been a surprise. She hadn't known her father had been in talks with the man or she would have delicately swayed the King away from Roussel.

This time she knew the King was looking for husbands for his unwed daughters.

This time she was doing something about it.

Elisabeth turned toward the window again and spotted Tristan once more. Her insides danced. She was beyond besotted with him.

Being wedded to Tristan would be heavenly.

Claire walked up behind her and wrapped her arms around Elisabeth's waist. Resting her chin on Elisabeth's shoulder, she said, "Why don't you tell him you love him?"

Her heart gave a hard thud. Elisabeth twisted around to face her sister. *"Pardon?"*

Claire dropped her arms to her sides and sighed. "Don't bother to deny it, Elisabeth. You're in love with Tristan de Tiersonnier. That is why we are here, isn't it? You want to wed him. That's the reason for the workers and gardeners. That is why you want Tristan reinstated—though I am not saying the other reasons aren't valid as well. You are trying to convince the King that Tristan is a suitable husband for you ."

Elisabeth was gripped by fear. "How—How did you—"

"Know? I've caught you looking at him, not just here, but at Versailles when he was Captain. It is the briefest of looks—in a way you don't look at any other man. Don't worry, Elisabeth. Tristan can't tell. No one can—except me. I'm your sister and I know you best of all. I'm the only one who sees it."

Elisabeth's heart pounded. "You'll swear to me, you'll not tell a soul. Do you hear me?"

"Of course I swear. I've known for some time and I've never breathed a word. I don't understand why you don't tell him of your affections. He seems to have grown quite fond of you. I don't think he'd find the notion of marrying you disagreeable. Discuss it with him, then with the King."

Lord, how naïve Claire was. Perhaps she'd sheltered her too much. "It isn't done that way. Nor is it that simple. You cannot embark upon any course of action without first reducing the chances of failure. Even if Tristan were agreeable, the King likely won't be. Walking up to His Majesty to request Tristan as my husband could and likely would be met with a resounding no. Then what? Once the King makes a decision, he'll not change it. The matter must be carefully handled, steps taken that are well thought out."

"Fine. Perhaps being more prudent with the King is a good idea, but why not tell Tristan how you feel?"

Elisabeth was aghast. "Are you mad? Claire, it is bad enough that I have done the unthinkable—fallen in love—when I know better. When I have seen the devastation that particular emotion causes women. We live at the whims of men. You know that. A woman under the influence of love who makes the mistake of declaring her affections pays the ultimate price. You know what happened to our mother when she professed her love to the King. Soon after, he became disenchanted and sent her away to the Convent of the Sacred Heart. This after she'd maintained his interest for *years*."

Claire lowered her gaze to the floor, looking doleful. The subject of their mother was difficult. Claire had been young and devastated when their mother had been sent away. Elisabeth had consoled her sister as best she could, despite her own broken heart.

Placing her hands on her sister's shoulders, Elisabeth sighed. She didn't want to distress Claire by bringing the subject up, but God help her, she had to be made to understand. "You mustn't ever wear your emotions on your sleeve." She squeezed Claire's shoulders. "You must remain guarded—with your thoughts and emotions. Never give anything away. Unless you wish to suffer. Unless you wish to lose the man you love."

Elisabeth had come to Tristan with the hope of ultimately purging him from her blood. It was now clear, it would take much longer than a week to accomplish.

It would take several lifetimes.

She hadn't wanted to love him so deeply, but she did. With all her heart. She always had.

She didn't want to lose him, and so she was forging ahead with her plan.

"I'm sorry, Elisabeth. You're right, of course." Her sister's eyes were large and sad.

Elisabeth hugged her. "You'll help me tomorrow, then?" She purposely changed the subject, not wanting to distress Claire further.

Claire pulled back, a small smile on her lips. "Yes. Whatever you need, I'll do."

"Good. We're going to show the King that Tristan is as capable as he always was to command the Guard."

Until today, Tristan had been avoiding his former men. Elisabeth could make no sense of it until Gabriel had confided that it was a matter of pride. She couldn't believe Tristan actually thought he'd been diminished by his injury. That he'd truly believe the King's foolish physicians and their ridiculous notions about his being unfit.

Or that Tristan would take to heart the King's misconceptions.

It only made Elisabeth want to see Tristan's reinstatement all the more.

There was only one man fit to command the King's elite corps, standing head and shoulders above any other candidate, and that was Tristan de Tiersonnier, Comte de Saint-Marcel.

The door opened. She pulled away from her sister and turned toward her visitor.

Tristan had walked into the room, filling it with his commanding presence.

Her heart swelled with joy.

Even with his cane, he still moved with a certain masculine grace that made her pulse quicken.

"Forgive me, I thought you were alone, Elisabeth." His rich sensual voice was like a warm caress down her spine. She loved how he spoke her name. There was such sinful promise to it. It swamped her senses and made her feel dangerously reckless and out of control. As much as that unnerved her, it also had a certain astonishing allure. At the moment, she could barely keep from throwing herself against his chiseled form and claiming his mouth.

"I was just leaving," Claire said after exchanging pleasantries with Tristan, and left the room.

A half-smile on his lips, he approached. Her insides danced with excitement. He stopped before her and slipped his fingers under her chin. "Have I kissed you good morning?" he asked.

She couldn't hold back her smile. "Yes." He'd done a lot more to her than kiss her that morning.

"Good. Because it's afternoon." Then his lips were against hers, his tongue possessing her mouth, and her arms by their own volition drew around him. She moaned.

She could make him a good wife. He would make her an excellent husband.

She'd failed to convince him to keep the workers and gardeners she'd sent, but she couldn't fail in any part of her plan tomorrow.

This hunt was too important.

So much hinged on its success. Briefly, she wondered if she should wear her lucky boots. Then Tristan's hand caressed the curve of her breast and her thoughts turned as heated as her body.

Chapter Six

Claire peered into the streaming river at the water's edge. "Have I told you how much I don't like this idea?"

The sun was high in the sky. Standing in the glen, Elisabeth could hear the voices and laughter coming from the King and his party as they drifted down into the narrow valley. The hunt had ended an hour ago. Elisabeth and her entourage had arrived just in time for the feasting and gaiety that were afoot.

Tristan was up there. It had taken well-placed words and kisses to convince him to join the escort that would take her to the picnic after the hunt—not that she minded the kissing. Or the amorous encounter that ensued. Only when she lay weak from the second intense orgasm in a row did he advise her—with the most devilish smile—that he'd had every intention of seeing her personally delivered to the hunt all along.

How could any woman be angry at a man who was so wickedly charming and had just melted her with his carnal talents?

"Yes, Claire, I believe you've mentioned it more than a dozen times."

Leaving his château that morning had been the most difficult thing she'd ever done. She'd come to adore the crumbling stony structure. It too had charmed her as much as its handsome lord. In short order, it had come to feel more like home than any place she'd ever lived.

Because within its walls there was Tristan.

Tristan made it home.

And she already missed being there with him. Already missed their daily strolls—each one lasting a little longer than the day before—and the horseback rides she'd coaxed him to take. Only the finest horsemen in the land could be part of the King's personal Guard. Tristan's skill was no exception. To her utmost joy his leg bothered him a little less each day. He didn't lean on his cane as much as before.

Then there were the wonderful picnics they'd had where he'd regaled her with stories about his military career. She'd hung on his every word—each battle he'd described, the concern and dread he'd felt. That he'd shared them with her meant more to her than he could ever imagine.

"Why do I have to be the one who falls into the river? Why can't it be you?" Claire complained.

"Because I'll look like a drowned rat. Not an enticing way for Tristan to see me."

Elisabeth's stomach had been in knots all day. And now as she stood with Claire, she was so nervous, her very entrails were quaking. This *had* to go well. She couldn't fail. She couldn't lose Tristan now.

Claire clamped her mouth shut, and frowning, glanced back at the river streaming past. "You think it's cold?"

"I'm sure it's not."

Claire shook her head. "This is definitely not going to be as much fun as the time you helped me hem nasty Cecile de Brun's gown up an inch each night to make her think she was growing at an alarming rate after she'd taunted me relentlessly about being short."

Elisabeth patted her sister's shoulder. "No time to reminisce about our girlhood pranks. You're a strong swimmer, Claire. You're going to be fine. I promise you, you won't be in the water long. Now then, Agathe is up there on the top of the glen to your left. Do you see her by the large walnut tree?"

"Yes," Claire said, spotting Elisabeth's trusted servant. Agathe stood well apart from the King's party. In point of fact, she was the only person in sight. The others were far from the edge of the glen.

"I will give Agathe the signal, then she will signal to you. When you see her nod, you jump in and start screaming. Tristan will be along shortly to save you."

"Fine," Claire said tightly. "Make certain he gets here quickly. I'm only doing this because I know you would do it for me."

"You know I'd do anything for you." Elisabeth's words rose from her heart.

"I hope this works, Elisabeth."

So did she.

*****

"The sex must be excellent." Gabriel smiled as he stood beside Tristan looking out at the royal gathering before him.

Tristan kept silent, ignoring his brother. He could clearly hear the mischief in his Gabriel's tone. Without glancing Gabriel's way, Tristan kept his gaze fixed on the crowd of men and women clustered in a giant group around the King, mostly praising His Majesty's abilities in the successful hunt.

Gabriel chuckled. "You heard me well, but I'll repeat myself nonetheless. I said, the sex must be quite good. You told me you wanted nothing to do with these people ever again and here you are, at the King's hunt—because of a woman."

Not just any woman. A very unique woman. Tristan had wanted never to see Versailles again. Now he wasn't so sure. There was someone at Versailles that he wanted to see a lot more of.

Elisabeth.

"She's the King's darling. I felt it necessary to escort her." Not to mention Tristan wanted to prolong his time with her. But he wasn't going to tell his brother that. He'd never hear the end of Gabriel's ribbing. Especially if he knew Tristan's interest in Elisabeth went beyond the physical.

Upon arriving with her entourage, she'd promptly brought him before the King. It pleased Tristan that His Majesty was glad to see him. Had seemed delightfully surprised, actually. Clearly, the King had expected Tristan to be far less mobile and agile. Tristan had exchanged pleasantries with him, then moved to the outer perimeter of the gathering, where he presently stood. A habit for a man whose job it was to keep a watchful eye from a distance, making certain he and his men maintained a safe radius around the King and his family at all times.

What dismayed him was that his replacement, Balzac, was mixing in with the group, parading about, usually at Veronique's side, when he should be maintaining a professional decorum. Just as disturbing were the sidelong glances and discreet smiles Veronique was giving Tristan. He knew what she was after. What message she was conveying. That he could fuck her if he wanted to, and she was doing this while Balzac panted at her side.

He couldn't believe that woman had ever held any kind of appeal.

"Sir."

Tristan glanced at the man addressing him. One of his former lieutenants, Valesque.

"It is good to see you, Commander," Valesque said.

"Not 'Commander,'" Tristan corrected.

"Of course. Forgive me. An old habit, I'm afraid. I hope you don't mind, but I wanted to tell you that the men and I are delighted to see you again."

Tristan glanced past Valesque's shoulder. Every Musketeer he could see, all standing well apart from the King's party, had their eyes on him. He looked at them one by one, as each gave a deep nod—an expression of respect.

"Lieutenant, tell your men to keep their eyes focused on the royal gathering," Tristan said. The men had a job to do and Tristan didn't want to be a distraction.

"Of course, Comm...er... sir. Sadly, that is an order that should be coming from Balzac, but I'm afraid he doesn't take matters seriously enough."

That was painfully obvious.

Valesque gave Tristan a short bow. "Good day, sir."

"Good day."

Valesque turned to leave.

"Lieutenant Valesque," Tristan called out.

The man turned back around.

"Please tell the men I'm delighted to see them also."

Valesque smiled. "Yes, sir. And, sir, when the men learned the Duchesse was in need of an escort to your château, well, suffice to say, it caused quite a commotion among the Musketeers. Every man wanted to be in the entourage that would escort Madame la Duchesse to your abode." Valesque gave him a bow and walked away.

Tristan felt his chest tighten. He was touched. And grateful to one very spirited, beautiful, favorite royal daughter.

Had she not come to his home, bold as could be, he'd likely still be in his château, feeling sorry for himself. She'd brought him back to life after he'd slipped into a dark hole. He'd enjoyed his time with her immensely. Not just in his bed. But her company in general.

He even delighted in providing her with lessons in fencing.

A smile tugged at the corners of his mouth as he remembered their second lesson. Determined not to drop her sword again, she'd shown up in the gardens, one of her silk scarves binding the blade to her hand. With determination etched on her lovely features—her goal, he knew, was to best him—she'd made improvements by leaps and bounds.

He loved her spiritedness—both in and out of bed.

Tristan scanned the crowd, looking for Elisabeth. She'd been with the King not long ago. Now she was nowhere to be found. The cooking fires were well in the distance surrounded by cooks hard at work preparing the meal. But he doubted Elisabeth would be there.

"Where are Elisabeth and Claire?" Gabriel, who'd been uncharacteristically silent, voiced the very question running through Tristan's mind.

Where could they be?

Moving his gaze from face to face in the distant throng, he suddenly spotted her emerging from the crowd. Smiling, she approached, looking far more alluring than any woman should. She made his heart race.

She stopped in front of him. "Are you enjoying yourselves, gentlemen?"

Since they'd become lovers, whenever she greeted him, she touched him. Though he understood why she couldn't at the moment, he hated it nonetheless that her hands were folded before her and not on him.

"I'm enjoying myself immensely," Gabriel answered with his usual smile.

"And what about you, Tristan? Are you enjoying yourself?"

He couldn't stop himself from luxuriating in the vision she made. In her pale gown, she looked ravishing. The décolletage accentuated her lovely breasts ever so deliciously. He was starved for the taste of her sweet nipples. Though he'd made love to her that morning, he wanted nothing more than to take her into the nearby forest and have her again. "I'd say the gathering has suddenly much improved now that you're here." Her presence would improve any gathering, regardless of how arduous it was.

"Why, thank you, Tristan." She blushed slightly, her eyes telling him his compliment pleased her. "I don't suppose either of you have seen my sister?"

Tristan frowned. "She wasn't with you?"

"No. I don't know where she is." Elisabeth tugged at her ear.

Tristan looked the crowd over again. "I don't see her."

"I wonder where she could be?" Gabriel said, scanning about, trying to spot her.

"I don't know. I'm a bit concerned. I haven't seen her for a while." Elisabeth tugged her ear again.

"Is there something wrong with your ear?" Tristan asked.

She dropped her arm down to her side. "No."

A scream ripped through the air. Tristan turned in the direction of the startling sound. More screams. They were coming from the glen.

Half running, half limping, he tore toward the edge. The moment he saw Claire flailing in the river below, his blood chilled. Vaguely, he heard Elisabeth's cry.

Without a thought, he ran down the hill as best he could, jarring pains stabbing through his leg along the way. Somehow he managed to reach the river's edge before anyone else. Somehow he'd made it without falling.

Tristan tossed down his cane, threw off his justacorps, and dove into the river after Claire. She was screaming and thrashing when he caught her around the waist. "It's all right, Claire. I have you." She quieted the moment he turned her onto her back. Swimming toward the shore, where Elisabeth and a number of Musketeers were waiting, Tristan pulled Claire to safety.

Arms reached out and dragged Claire out of the water. Two of the men lay Claire carefully down onto the grass, while two others pulled Tristan onto the shore.

Elisabeth was at her sister's side in an instant. Dropping to her knees, she threw her arms around her and wept against her sister's cheek.

Tristan rose and accepted his cane from one of his former men. Raking a hand through his wet hair, he glanced up to the top of the glen. The King and the rest of the gathering stood in a line, witness to what had transpired.

The crowd burst into applause.

His Majesty locked gazes with Tristan and gave him a simple nod of thanks.

Just then Balzac came racing down to the shore line.

Elisabeth shot to her feet. "Where were you!" she shouted at him.

Balzac, two years Tristan's senior, stopped short. He glanced up at the audience on the top of the glen, then back at Elisabeth.

"My sister could have drowned!" she continued. "Are you or are you not responsible for the safety and well-being of the royal family?"

Balzac looked gray, clearly embarrassed by the very public dressing-down. "Y-Yes, madame, I am."

"And yet it was left to the Comte de Saint-Marcel"—she gestured at Tristan—"to rescue my sister because you were nowhere to be found."

Balzac tossed a nervous glance at the King. "Madame, perhaps one should examine what your sister was doing in the river in the first place."

Tristan mentally cringed. That was an imbecilic mistake. Balzac's comment suggested Claire was to blame for ending up in the river. One didn't blame members of the King's family for anything—whether they were at fault or not.

Elisabeth placed her hands on her waist and jutted out her chin. "I'll tell you what she was doing. She was *drowning* in it—while you, sir, were enjoying the fresh summer air." She turned toward two Musketeers. "Please take my sister to my carriage." As Claire was being helped away, Elisabeth turned to Tristan.

"Thank you for saving Claire."

Tristan noted that Elisabeth didn't have any tears in her eyes. Nor did her eyes look red from crying—even though she'd been sobbing against her sister. She spun on her heels, grabbed her skirts and marched up the hill to the top of the glen, straight for her father, glimpses of black boots appearing and disappearing as her skirts swayed.

Jésus-Christ, she was wearing her boots beneath her gown.

Tristan couldn't shake the feeling in his gut. One that suggested all was not as it appeared.

*****

"Go ahead and say it . . . I was brilliant." Claire smiled. Back in Versailles, in Claire's private rooms, Elisabeth sat on the edge of Claire's bed, holding her sister's hand.

"You were brilliant." Elisabeth smiled warmly at her. "I am forever grateful."

"Well, it was worth it. I think it worked. Did you see Balzac when you yelled at him? I think he may have soiled his breeches." Claire burst into a fit of giggles, her laughter contagious. She added as soon as she was sober enough to speak, "Veronique's face was precious. She was scowling, furious over the spectacle made of her lover."

"He is completely unfit to hold such an esteemed position as Captain of the King's private Guard. He is incompetent. I told the King as much."

Claire sat up, her eyes wide. "And? What did the King say? Is he going to dismiss him?"

Elisabeth sighed. "I don't know. I know he was impressed by Tristan. It is heartening that he insisted Tristan return to the palace with the rest of us. At this point, I will remain guardedly optimistic."

Her father had allowed her only a few private words after the river incident. The King was a difficult man to read. She had no idea what he was thinking. Or what he wished to do.

Moreover, she had the added problem of Veronique. Elisabeth hadn't missed the sultry looks she'd cast Tristan today. Veronique would shamelessly welcome both Balzac and Tristan into her bed. One of them was sure to be Captain of the Guard, and she wanted to make certain that man was her lover. She'd aggressively chase Tristan if she needed to.

A sudden knock at the door snatched Elisabeth from her thoughts.

Agathe entered with a member of the King's Guard. "Madame, this gentleman wishes to speak to you."

The Musketeer stepped into the room and bowed. "Madame, mademoiselle," he greeted. "The King has summoned both of you. He wishes to see you straightaway."

Elisabeth rose. Her stomach clenched. Claire was being summoned, too? A cold sense of foreboding sank its teeth into her. She didn't like the sound of this. She couldn't quell her unease.

*****

With a smile fixed to her face and a strong and steady stride, Elisabeth entered the Hall of Mirrors and made her way to the opposite end. Though she'd lectured Claire en route about walking with confidence, Claire scurried along beside her looking every bit like a frightened mouse. At the end of the long corridor, His Majesty, Veronique and Tristan awaited them. Seeing Veronique looking spiteful was no surprise. But seeing Tristan standing to the King's left beside her half-sister unbalanced Elisabeth.

Feeding her trepidation was the fact that the Hall of Mirrors was empty, and the doors that led to the gardens, closed. The Hall of Mirrors was always filled with courtiers and Musketeers. That the King wanted a private audience unsettled her further.

By the time Elisabeth reached the end of the long hall, her anxiety had swelled considerably, leaving her legs feeling wobbly.

She and Claire stopped before the King and curtsied low.

"Your Majesty," Elisabeth said, thankful that her voice hadn't quavered. Standing before his solid silver throne, several carpeted steps above her, her father looked every bit the monarch of the most powerful nation in all of Christendom, his tall red-heeled shoes lending to his grandeur.

Elisabeth could see Tristan from the corner of her eye. His expression was tight and unreadable.

"Go ahead and admit the truth." Veronique stepped toward Elisabeth.

Elisabeth turned to Veronique. "The truth?" she responded coolly, though the pounding of her heart was so hard and fierce now, she worried the others could hear it.

"Yes. Tell the King that today's 'drowning' was contrived, meant to fool His Majesty."

Claire shifted her weight next to her, her nervousness tangible. Yet Elisabeth gave no indication of her agitation and dragged her gaze away from Veronique and to her father. Dear God, Veronique was making yet another attempt to ruin her before the King.

"Your Majesty," Elisabeth began. "I have no idea of what she speaks."

"Your Majesty," Veronique injected.

The King silenced her by raising a hand. "Elisabeth, Veronique is under the impression that you are scheming, trying to have Balzac removed as Captain of the Musketeers."

Elisabeth gave a mirthless laugh. "I don't need to scheme, Sire. Balzac does a poor enough job to have himself removed as Captain of the Guard."

"Claire," the King called out, making Claire jump. "Tell me how you ended up in the river."

To Claire's credit, she lifted her chin and met the King's gaze. "I . . . I was refreshing myself when I slipped and fell in."

"She's lying," Veronique accused. "She'd say anything, do anything, to protect Elisabeth, Sire. I saw how Tristan de Tiersonnier looked at Elisabeth today. You sent her to him to obtain an instructor for fencing—a ridiculous pastime for a woman, I might add." Veronique tossed Elisabeth a hateful look. "I believe while she was there, they became lovers. It's obvious that Elisabeth is plotting, trying to ensure that her lover holds the esteemed position as the commander of the Musketeers."

"That's amusing coming from a woman who beds Balzac," Elisabeth drawled.

Veronique opened her mouth, clearly intent on venting her outrage, but the King intervened. "Enough!" He turned to Tristan. "Tristan, you have never lied to me. I want the truth from your lips. Are you Elisabeth's lover?"

Elisabeth could scarcely breathe. She couldn't look at Tristan, afraid her strong emotions for him would somehow be detected.

"Yes, Your Majesty."

Elisabeth's stomach plummeted.

"I see." The King's response was tight.

Terror gripped her. The last thing she wanted was for Tristan to be punished in any way. She wouldn't allow him or her sister to pay for her mistakes and miscalculations. This was all her doing. The entire muddled mess. Her plans had always helped her and Claire. Elisabeth had become a master at them, successfully countering the constant jostling and plotting that were so a part of court life.

And she was good at it. It was all she knew. All she knew how to do in the circumstances she lived in.

There was only one thing she could do to protect Tristan and Claire and keep Veronique from succeeding with her plan to discredit and diminish her before the King—and that was to sacrifice her own plan.

What choice did she have?

Her chest immediately tightened in anguish. She fought back tears, knowing how dangerous it would be to shed a single one.

"Your Majesty," Elisabeth said, forcing the words from her lips despite the knot in her throat, "I attended Tristan de Tiersonnier's château with two intentions. The first was to obtain lessons in fencing from the greatest swordsman in the realm. The second was to bed him. I find him appealing and I seduced him." She tilted her head to one side. "Surely this doesn't surprise you, Sire? After all, such appetites are in our blood. In our very nature, Your Majesty. And the opposite sex simply cannot resist our charms. No?"

The words were like poison in her mouth. She felt ill having to reduce what she'd shared with Tristan to meaningless carnal moments—an empty conquest—when each kiss and touch had meant so much more.

Tristan stiffened, but he held his tongue.

The King studied her for a moment. Her heart pounded in her throat. Then his lips twitched and he tossed his head back in laughter. "Ah, dear Elisabeth. There are times I believe you should have been born a male." He descended the steps chuckling, and then offered his arm. She took it, and somehow maintained her smile, though her heart was fragmenting into a million sharp, piercing shards.

"You are correct, daughter," her father said to her, leading her out toward the gardens. "It is in our nature to crave and enjoy decadent delights."

"But—But what about—" Veronique began.

"That will be all on the subject, Veronique," their father tossed over his shoulder, not bothering to glance Veronique's way.

Elisabeth couldn't look at Tristan. Keeping her eyes straight ahead, she let the King lead her outside into a throng of waiting courtiers, her heartache keen and suffocating. She'd thwarted her half-sister and managed to retain the King's favor. Claire would be all right. As would Tristan. She'd managed to quell any ire the King may have had toward him as well.

But it had cost her dearly. She'd lost Tristan. He was an honorable man, honest and true—qualities she loved about him. He favored those qualities in others. She knew he despised those who deceived and schemed. She'd just confirmed in his heart and mind—with her own words—that his original perception of her was right—she was a hollow schemer, spoiled and looking for diversions.

Worse, for all her bravado, deep inside she was a coward. A woman who didn't have the courage to speak the truth, let down her guard, and expose her true emotions to the man she loved to mend matters between them.

CHAPTER SEVEN

Elisabeth stared out the window of her private apartments at the palace the next day. Her eyes felt raw from lack of sleep and copious tears. Pacing most of the night, she'd thought of different things she could say to mend matters with Tristan. All of which were foolish. None of which professed her love. By morning she'd come to the conclusion that though she had the ability to give Tristan her body, she'd no ability to voice the words burning in her heart for him—knowing full well that if she tried to voice those three words, they'd lodge in her throat.

How was she to undo the training and ingraining she'd been subjected to her entire life? She had no idea how to wrestle down her fear of laying herself bare. Of making herself vulnerable emotionally. It was irrational, yet gripping and real.

Besides, she had no confidence at all that Tristan would even believe her if she tried to explain everything and told him she how much she loved him.

By early afternoon, Elisabeth didn't have to torture herself any longer. Agathe had advised her that Tristan was gone, his rooms at Versailles vacated.

She swiped away a tear and rested her head against the window. Depending on who her father chose as her next husband, she may never see Tristan again. Not even so much as a passing glance.

The door to her antechamber swung open and slammed shut. She jumped and spun around. Tristan walked toward her, his cane in hand, taking her by surprise. Looking so beautiful.

A stab of longing pierced her heart.

He stopped mere feet from her. "Let me see if I understand this correctly. You convinced your father to send you to my château for a fencing instructor, intending while you were there to get me to bed you. Is that accurate?" His tone was matter-of-fact. She didn't know what to make of it or his presence.

"Answer me, Elisabeth," he insisted.

She clasped her hands and looked down.

"Yes," she responded softly.

"Then you decided to attend the King's hunt, when you don't like the hunts, convinced your sister she should jump into the river so I could save her, look like a hero, and reclaim my former position as Captain of the King's private Guard. Is that correct?"

Oh, God. "I . . ."

He hooked her arm with his cane and yanked her to him. She collided against him with a gasp. Her palms were suddenly flat against his sculpted chest. Slipping his fingers under her chin, he tilted it up. "I've obtained answers from Claire. I'll have answers from you, too. Now then, I'm going to ask you again: did you contrive the incident at the river yesterday just so I could be reinstated?"

Clearly, Claire had confessed. What was the point of denying it? This was going badly. Anguished, she didn't have any fight in her today. Being this close to Tristan, and knowing he wouldn't kiss her or touch her the way she longed for, was torturous.

"Yes" was all she could muster past her lips.

"You think I needed your help in returning to the Guard?"

She looked into his eyes and said firmly, "No. You are highly skilled and respected. If you wanted to return, you'd succeed. You don't need help from me." She meant that. It was no lie.

His features and voice softened. "There you are wrong."

"Pardon?" she asked, perplexed.

"After the injury, I was filled with bitterness. Anger. I was not myself at all. I might have been that way indefinitely had you not arrived and wedged yourself into my life."

Speechless, she simply blinked, surprised by his answer.

He released her chin and shook his head. "When the King dismissed me from my post as the Captain of the Musketeers, I made no attempt to speak to him about his decision. I simply left, reeling from the sting of it. I should have spoken to him then. I should have told him that, injury or not, I am still capable of commanding the Guard. Your antics yesterday inspired a conversation with him. A conversation that was long overdue. And I have you to thank for it. Who knows if or when I would have stopped brooding like a fool and talked to King." The smile formed in his eyes before one touched lightly upon his lips. "I have been reinstated as the Captain of his Guard."

Her eyes widened. "Truly? What about Balzac?"

"Veronique will be marrying Balzac and leaving the palace with him. He is being given lands to take away any sting *he* may feel from being replaced."

She smiled, overcome with joy for him. "I'm so very happy for you, Tristan."

He caressed her cheek with the back of his knuckles. "You didn't look very happy when I walked in. In fact, you look like you've been crying. Tell me…why did you want me reinstated? Why did you want me to have you? Why have you gone to such lengths where I'm concerned?" His tone was as gentle as his touch. "We both know the answer. Speak the words, Elisabeth. Let me hear you say them."

Her breaths slipped past her parted lips, shallow and sharp. Old familiar fears welled inside her and tightened around her throat like a vise. Unable to summon the words, they remained trapped inside her.

"Elisabeth, at the risk at sounding immodest, I have had a woman or two in love with me in the past. As clever as you are, some things are impossible to hide. Especially during and after sex. Tender looks, tender touches point clearly to tender emotions."

Tears stung her eyes.

"You've spent a lifetime suppressing every emotion that would leave you exposed and susceptible. You're afraid to be open and vulnerable"

Was it written on her forehead? Just how obvious was she to this man?

He slipped his fingers beneath her chin again. "You're trembling. You can't say it, can you?"

She lowered her eyes. Part of her wanted to so badly.

He lifted her chin, capturing her gaze. "Repeat after me: *Tristan.*"

He wasn't serious?

"It's just my name, Elisabeth. You've said it many times before." The start of a smile pulled at the corners of his beautiful mouth. "At times you've even screamed it as you were coming. Let's hear it now, Elisabeth. *Tristan.*"

She took in a ragged breath and ceded. "Tristan."

"I."

She remained silent.

"*I,*" he pressed.

"I."

"Love."

Elisabeth swallowed hard against the lump constricting her throat. "L-Love."

He smiled. "You."

A tear slipped down her cheek. "*You* . . . so very much!" The words tumbled from her mouth, surprising her.

His smile turned into a grin. "Excellent. Now then, let's continue: *Tristan*—Say it."

"T-Tristan . . ."

"I want you to be my husband."

Tears flooding her eyes were making it difficult to see his cherished face. "I want you to be my husband," she said, the words flowing out of her mouth, unhindered.

"Because I can't live without you."

Quietly, she wept. "Be-Because I can't live without you."

He brushed a curl off her damp cheek. "That wasn't so difficult, was it?"

She shook her head no. "Yes."

He tossed his head back and laughed. "Elisabeth, you are one of a kind, *ma chérie*." He gave her a soft kiss. A warm quiver shimmered down her spine.

He broke the kiss, leaving her wanting more.

Now that you've agreed to marry me," he said, "I suppose I should tell you that my conversation with His Majesty included the subject of your future husband." Dipping his head, he whispered in her ear, "You will be my wife."

Her knees almost gave out. It was all too incredible. So glorious! She stepped back, stunned. "How—How did you convince him? What did you say?"

"That I am the best man for you and he should give the man who saved his life and the life of his daughter, Princess Claire, the hand of his favorite offspring."

Oh, how she loved him!

"There is one more thing I want to hear you say." He cradled her cheek in his palm. "Tristan, I really want you to . . ."

She was beaming now. "Tristan, I really want you to . . ."

He leaned in and brushed his lips along her neck, sending shivers of delight through her. "Make love to me right now and every day for the rest of our lives."

She laughed. And cried. And reeled with happiness. "Make love to me right now . . . and every day . . . for the rest of our lives."

That devilish grin she adored spread across his lips. "Now there's a request I can't deny."

Then he led her to the bedchamber, her body heating up every step of the way. Once inside, they stripped away their clothing posthaste, and he tossed her onto the bed, his urgency snatching away her breath.

The press of his naked form against the length of her body was sublime. Her hungry core clenched and creamed, eager for him. He had her mouth, claiming it. Famished, she sucked his tongue into her mouth, thrilled by his groan.

His hand skimmed along her skin from her shoulder to her breast, a fiery path straight to her taut nipple. He pinched it, holding it captive between his fingers until it began to throb, a delicious pulsing sensation that radiated from her breast and echoed in her sex. She arched and writhed, delirious with need, her body on fire. He released her nipple and sucked it into his hot mouth, his wicked fingers capturing her other nipple, treating it to the same sweet torture. The sound of pleasure shot up her throat, the double stimulation on the sensitized tips almost too much to take.

"Please," she panted. "I want you now."

"I'm going to come inside you," he rasped against the pulsating tip of her breast. "Do you understand me? I'm not pulling my cock out."

All she could do was moan. The thought of him filling her with his essence made her hotter. Wetter. "Yes. Do it."

Tristan filled her sex with one solid thrust. She wrapped her legs around him. He wanted to howl with pleasure, love and lust burning inside him with equal intensity. He couldn't believe it when Claire had told him Elisabeth had loved him from afar for so long. He couldn't believe the touching lengths she'd gone to just to be with him.

And he was going to spend a lifetime returning her love. Cherishing her every day.

"*Dieu*, I love you." He pumped his hips, hitting the sweet spot on her clit with his every downstroke. "I can't get enough of you."

"I love you!" She was breathless and so wet, her cream was seeping from around his thick cock. "I love you, Tristan."

She was already on the edge, and *Jésus-Christ*, so was he.

"Come for me . . . Come with me."

Her body tensed. "Oh! I'm coming!"

Tristan gathered her tightly in his arms and rode her for all he was worth, fighting back his release, waiting for hers to hit so he could let go. He felt the tremor in her sheath, her body arch. And with her scream of rapture, he held nothing back. His come shot down his length. In shuddering waves he poured his prick into her quivering cunt in hot steady streams, driving his cock as deeply as he could with each powerful thrust. Overwhelmed by her orgasm, she moaned and whimpered, clenching all around him, her arms, her legs, her sex, sending a growl rumbling from his chest. He'd never known such stunning pleasure, such pure ecstasy, as the mind-numbing joy it was to drain himself inside her.

With her now quiet in his arms and his prick emptied, he reluctantly withdrew.

Tristan looked down at her. There was a smile in her eyes. She lifted her head off the bed, cupped his cheek, and gave him a warm kiss. He'd just come inside her, claimed her for his own, and yet she said with a lazy grin and a soft sigh, "You're mine."

Tristan couldn't hold back his own grin. He nuzzled her neck. Breathed her name. "And you are mine," he assured her.

He'd never met anyone like Elisabeth. She was the only woman he knew who could drive him wild in a pair of breeches and the most irregular boots he'd ever seen.

She made him feel like the richest man on earth. The luckiest man in the realm.

Tristan had won the heart and hand of the fair princess.

HISTORICAL TIDBIT

Musketeers were NOT the fools with blades you've seen in the movies.

These men were highly trained and seriously skilled. To make it into the King's private Guard—the Musketeers—to be responsible for the safety of the monarch and royal family, and entrusted to deliver sensitive messages across enemy lines during the many battles France fought as they worked to increase their nation (the largest in all of Christendom during the seventeenth century), you had to not only be the best of the best when it came to horsemanship, and wielding weapons, but of noble birth, too.

These men were an elite corps. Men you wouldn't mess with.

And yet, there was a certain woman who gave them considerable grief. :)

Her name was Julie d'Aubigny (a.k.a. *la Maupin*)—an extraordinary swordswoman who bloody well lived her life by her own rules! Elisabeth, my heroine in BEWITCHING IN BOOTS, was inspired by her. The moment I read about *la Maupin*, I knew I had to create a character similar to her.

Julie's father was the Grand Squire of France, responsible for the royal stables and training King Louis XIV's pages. And he made sure his daughter trained right alongside them. From a young age, Julie learned fencing, horseback riding, and how to deliver a fist in the face if you were too stupid not to back off when threatened.

She grew up to be beautiful, took any lover she fancied, knew how to take care of herself—and often donned men's clothing when it suited her. Dressed in male attire, she attended taverns where Musketeers were known to frequent, just to provoke a duel with one of them. Once she had the Musketeer on the ground, defeated, she'd whip off her male disguise and made darn sure they knew it was a *woman* who'd bested a member of the King's prestigious Guard.

And Louis XIV loved it! He was so amused by stories of Julie's antics that he would often ask about her. One day the King was informed by one of his advisors that Julie had been arrested, "for dueling, Your Majesty."

The King immediately demanded, "Read me the law."

A very confused advisor promptly provided the legal authority for Julie's arrest. "Right here, Sire. It says, *"No man shall duel..."*

"That's correct. No *man* shall duel. She is a woman. Let her go." He'd given her carte blanche to do as she pleased with his personal Guard.

The glittering court of Louis XIV was as salacious as it was elegant. It was during this time period that the father of fairy tales, Charles Perrault—author of *The Tales of Mother Goose*— wrote stories that have delighted generations: *Sleeping Beauty, Little Red Riding Hood, Puss in Boots, Bluebeard* and the ever popular, *Cinderella,* to name a few.

I hope you enjoyed your time in the world when fairy tales were born. Please see the end for a delicious excerpt of yet another Fiery Tale!

Happy reading!

GLOSSARY

Antechamber—The sitting room in a lord's or lady's private apartments (chambers).

Caleçons—Drawers/underwear.

Chambers—Another word for private apartments. A lord's or lady's chambers consisted of a bedroom, a sitting room, a bathroom, and a *cabinet* (office). Some chambers were bigger and more elaborate than others. Some *cabinets* were so large, they were used for private meetings.

Chère—Endearment for a woman (*cher* for a man). Meaning: *dear one.*

Chérie—Endearment for a woman *(chéri* for a man). Meaning: *darling* or *cherished one.*

Comte—Count.

Comtesse—Countess.

Dieu—*God.*

Duc—Duke.

Duchesse—Duchess.

Hôtel—*A mansion located in the city.* The upper class and the wealthy bourgeois (middle class) often had a mansion in Paris (hôtel) in addition to their palatial country estates (château).

Justacorps – A fitted knee-length coat, worn over a man's vest and breeches.

Merde—*Shit.*

Salle de Buffet—*Dining Room.*

READ AN EXCERPT OF
THE MARQUIS'S NEW CLOTHES

Inspired by the tale of The Emperor's New Clothes, an erotically charged historical romance novella from the acclaimed Fiery Tales series that would have made Hans Christian Andersen blush.

There is a certain gorgeous lord who's quite difficult to resist...

To save her cousin, Aimee de Miran must retrieve a jeweled ring from the most sinfully seductive man at court, the unsuspecting Marquis de Nattes. But to search his considerable wardrobe she'll have to get very close to the notorious rake...and remain immune to his intoxicating charm.

But without his clothes—well, that's completely impossible.

Adam de Nattes has secretly burned for his best friend's wife for years. Now that Aimee is a widow, now that he's discovered her in his bedchambers, he intends to get very close to her indeed— with his clothes—and hers—utterly forgotten...

***Originally published in THE PRINCESS IN HIS BED anthology.

CHAPTER ONE

"My life is over!" Louise d'Arcy exclaimed the moment after she'd yanked Aimee inside her elegant private apartments and slammed the door shut.

Aimee de Miran sighed. She'd just arrived at Versailles. Her sojourn at the palace was only ten minutes long and already she was rethinking her plan to attend court and visit with her cousin.

Dear Louise was always in the midst of chaos. It seemed now was no different.

Parched from the long carriage ride, Aimee walked over to the pitcher of water and orange slices on the ebony side table and promptly filled two crystal goblets. "Louise, darling, I'm certain your life isn't over." She held a goblet out to her cousin. "Now why don't you tell me what's wrong."

"What's wrong? Renault is what's wrong. He's cast me aside!" Wringing her hands, Louise began to pace, completely oblivious to Aimee's extended arm and the goblet of fresh water being offered.

Aimee availed herself of the refreshment instead and set the goblet down.

A lovers' spat. Nothing new.

"I see." That would be all she'd need to say for the next hour while Louise ranted. When she was done, her cousin would collapse in a chair, quite theatrically, and weep for at least twenty more minutes.

Aimee had been through this before. Many times. Louise was always having spats with her longtime lover, Renault de Sard.

Louise stopped dead in her tracks. "No, you don't see. You've no idea what has occurred. Everything is a mess. And it's over this time! Truly over!" Her hazel eyes filled with tears. "He'll not have anything more to do with me. He's said so!" She dropped her face into her palms and sobbed.

Aimee approached and put a consoling arm around her cousin. Of similar age, they'd always been close. She did adore Louise, despite her histrionics. "Louise, it will work out. You'll see. He always comes back."

"Not this time," she said without lifting her head, the words muffled by her hands.

"You say that every time."

Her cousin's head shot up. "This time it's true!"

"You say *that* every time, too."

Louise let out a sharp breath. "Aimee, he favors another! I have been replaced. He's with Diane de Millon. I'm no longer his mistress at all! I tell you, he is a horrible, *horrible* cad! He purposely misled me."

"Oh? Misled you how?"

"I was positively thrilled when he asked me to accompany him to the palace for his regular official visit with the King. He'd been so cold and distant lately that I didn't think he'd permit me to attend this time. In truth, his plan was to bring me here to end our affair. He thought I wouldn't pitch a fit at the palace. And do you know what I did?"

"You pitched a fit at the palace."

"No. Well . . . yes." Louise waved her hand dismissively. "But that was in private. And that's not what I'm talking about." Her cousin began to pace and wring her hands again. "I did something. Something terrible. Something I regret."

Trepidation was beginning to mount in Aimee. Louise always had a flare for the dramatic, but . . . Aimee couldn't shake the disquieting feeling tightening in her stomach. There was a certain look in Louise's eyes that made her a little anxious.

"What did you do?"

Her cousin smoothed her hands down her gown. A habit. Something Louise always did when she was nervous. Or uneasy. Or terribly guilty.

"Well, you see . . ." Louise began and smoothed her hands down her gown again. "You must understand, I was quite angry with Renault at the time, and very hurt by his cutting coldness toward me. So I . . ."

Aimee braced herself. Having no idea what she was about to hear, her instincts told her it was going to be bad. Quite bad. "You *what?*"

"I took something of his."

"Took?"

"All right, I *stole.* There, I said it. Is that better? I *stole* something he holds dear."

Good Lord. This was a new low, even for Louise. "What on earth did you steal?"

Louis threw up her hands. "The man has never given me *anything*, Aimee. In all these years, no lover's trinket. No jewelry at all! I felt he owed me at least that much."

Aimee struggled with her patience. "Louise . . . What. Did. You. Take?"

"His jeweled ring. One of the ones given to him by the King."

"Oh, Louise, you didn't."

"I did!" Louise flopped down onto the nearby chair dropped her face into her palms again, and wept audibly.

Aimee shook her head, dismayed. Of all the predicaments Louise had landed herself in, this one was by far the most shocking. "Didn't it occur to you that Renault is the King's Lieutenant General of Police? A man who is overzealous when it comes to the duties of his post and would arrest his own mother for the most minor infraction?"

Louise looked up. "Well, not at the time, but it certainly has over the last few hours . . ." She choked on a sob. "What am I going to do? My life is over! He'll throw me in one of those horrible cells without batting an eye. If he's angry enough, he could have orders drawn up against me, and I'll be held without trial—for who knows how long."

Aimee took in a fortifying breath and let it out slowly. She walked over to her distressed kin and placed a hand on her shoulder. "Everything is going to be fine. We can remedy this problem. This really isn't as great a dilemma as you think it is."

Her cousin swiped away the tears on her cheek. "Oh, but it is."

"No it isn't. You will return the ring with a sincere apology–"

"I can't."

"You're right. The man is so rigid and uncompromising, he won't understand," Aimee said as an idea occurred to her. "I have it. You'll sneak into his rooms and put the ring back, without him being the wiser."

"I can't do that either."

Aimee frowned. "What do you mean, you can't?"

"I lost the ring."

"You *what?*"

Louise rose from the chair. "Well, it's not entirely lost. I know where it is. Sort of."

"Where in the name of God is it—*sort of?*"

"I had it with me when I was in the Hall of Mirrors yesterday. It was very crowded, as usual. I was bumped from behind, and it fell out of my hand and into the pocket of one of the courtiers."

"Do you know who?"

"I do. The Marquis de Nattes."

Aimee's heart missed a beat. "Adam de Vey, Marquis de Nattes?" she questioned, hoping she'd heard wrong.

"Yes. Exactly." Her cousin grasped Aimee's hands and squeezed them. "Aimee, I can't let Renault learn what I did. If the ring is found on the Marquis de Nattes's person, Renault would never believe he stole the ring. He has one of his own from the King. You must help me get the ring back before Renault discovers it missing. He'll not stop until he uncovers the thief. Me!"

This was only getting worse. She didn't like the direction this conversation was taking. "What exactly are you suggesting I do?"

For the first time since Aimee entered the room, her cousin smiled. "You know as well as I do the Marquis de Nattes would be receptive to any attention you would give him. Since Marc died, he looks at you 'that' way. You could easily get close enough to him to search his clothes."

Aimee's brows shot up. "Have you gone mad? You want me to encourage that libertine just so I can dip my hands in his pockets in search of your ring?"

"Precisely. And perhaps you can search his armoire in his private apartments, too. The man does have a rather extensive wardrobe . . ."

"No. Absolutely not." Adam de Vey was the worst sort of man. The very type she detested. He was no different than her late husband. Beautiful as sin. A master at seduction.

And completely faithless.

A man who believed women were interchangeable. Who cared nothing of what he did to a woman's heart. Only what he did with her body.

It was no wonder that the Marquis de Nattes and her late husband, Marc, Comte de Gremont, had been friends. They were of like mind and poor character. Since Marc's death on the dueling field three years ago—a duel over his favorite paramour at the time—Aimee thankfully had had nothing more to do with her late husband's licentious friends.

Louise's bottom lip began to tremble, her eyes welling with fresh tears. "Renault will show me no mercy. He cares nothing for me at all now. If—If you don't help me . . . then I will surely be arrested, Aimee. You won't let that happen, will you? You'll help me, won't you?"

The pitiful look on her cousin's face tugged at Aimee's heart fiercely. She wanted to help her, but . . . she'd noticed the lingering looks Adam had given her since Marc's death, too. The last thing she wanted to do was to make him believe she'd be receptive to him.

"Louise . . . There's got to be another way . . ."

"There isn't! Oh, please, Aimee. I haven't anyone else who can help . . . I know you don't care for Adam de Vey, but think of it this way: You can do something most women cannot. You can easily flirt with Adam, yet resist him, and in the end do what no female has done—rebuff him."

Now, that did have a certain appeal. Men like the Marquis de Nattes toyed with so many women, luring them with their polished manner, potent sensuality, their false affections. She would definitely love to play him. Lure him. She could flirt a little. Draw close enough to locate the ring and save Louise.

She was likely one of the few women in the realm who'd resist his allure.

After giving herself over to her husband—heart, body, and soul—leaving herself open to the humiliation and heartbreak she'd ultimately endured, Aimee knew she'd never fall into the arms of another rake like Marc again.

"All right," tumbled from her mouth.

Louise squeaked with joy and threw her arms around Aimee. "Thank you! I knew I could count on your help."

Aimee sighed. "I don't suppose you have any idea what he was wearing when you dropped the ring?"

"I do!" Louise was finally smiling again. "He was wearing a blue justacorps."

"Blue? That's it?"

"I know how much the man adores fine clothing, and I did hear he had a new wardrobe delivered two days ago, but really, how many blue justacorps could he have in all?"

True. But given the number of knee-length coats he owned, what were the chances he'd wear the same blue justacorps again anytime soon? Just how mindful was he of such things?

"Between the two of us, we'll be able to locate the ring quickly and easily," Louise said confidently.

Aimee couldn't believe she'd become embroiled in this mad plan. Outfoxing a seasoned roué; locating and lifting a ring out from under the nose of a man who, by his very womanizing nature, was highly attuned to the opposite sex. Reading women was his forte. He knew how to detect signs of amorous interest and sexual desire. Her performance would have to be believable and flawless, despite her limited skills at being a coquette.

Success hinged on her ability to stay focused. The problem was, she hadn't been touched by a man in over three long empty years. Though she'd never admit it to anyone, she yearned to have a man's arms around her. The press of his hard body against hers. His body inside her. Her marriage bed had been most satisfying. Too satisfying. There had been many nights she wished her late husband had never introduced her to the pleasures of sex. That his conjugal visits had been more typical of his peers—brief. Obligatory. For the purposes of procreation only.

Awakening her to physical delights had caused her nothing but suffering.

For many reasons.

But no matter how much she desired a lover, she *wouldn't* take a man like the Marquis de Nattes to satisfy her carnal cravings.

For Louise's sake, Aimee had to succeed. She couldn't fail. She *would* best Adam in this cat and mouse game they were about to play.

And she was going to use his libertine nature to her advantage.

*****

Adam de Vey, Marquis de Nattes, surveyed the various justacorps—fitted knee-length coats of various fabrics and colors. He'd had a second armoire placed in his private rooms to hold his recently arrived new clothes.

Doors to both armoires were open wide as he decided on his attire for the afternoon. The news of Aimee's arrival made his selection a little more important. Made his heart beat faster, and his blood course hotter just knowing she was close by.

Adam couldn't believe his luck. Just when he'd reached his breaking point. Just when he'd been racking his mind, trying to orchestrate an opportunity to spend time under the same roof with the dark-haired beauty, she fortuitously showed up at the palace. He'd no idea when he'd been summoned by the King for an official meeting that she'd be in attendance at Versailles as well.

It was a good sign. A great sign. Somehow the stars had aligned and he was getting what he'd been wishing for for years. Access to Aimee. She wouldn't be able to leave anytime soon either. The King took personal offense to brief visits at the palace.

Her stay would have to be no less than half a month. Plenty of time for him to do something he'd dreamed about far too often.

Bedding her.

It was going to be a challenge—his very first when it came to seducing a woman.

Dressed in black breeches and a white linen shirt, he watched as his loyal servant pulled out yet another justacorps, this one gold-colored, and brought it to him.

Adam touched the silk sleeve. "Not this one, Laurent," he said. Too bold.

The man, ten years his senior, returned the gold overcoat to the armoire.

"Really, Adam, I don't understand your interest in all these clothes." Reclining in a plush chair, his fingers laced behind his head, his friend Robert, Comte de Senville, smiled.

"I like the finer things in life. Fine clothes. A fine château. Fine women." Aimee de Miran was by far the finest he'd ever laid eyes on.

"How is this, my lord?" Laurent held before him a red justacorps.

Also bold. "I don't think so."

He was looking for something more understated. A quiet elegance. Just like Aimee.

"All this trouble for a tumble. Don't think I don't know you're planning on seducing Aimee de Miran. And it's about time, I say." Chuckling, Robert crossed his arms over his chest and shook his head. "Six years . . . *Dieu!*"

Adam placed his hands on his hips, cursing the night he'd gotten drunk last month and let it slip to Robert about his longtime fascination with their dead friend's wife.

Ignoring Robert's irksome remarks was easier than ignoring his own hardened cock—his body's natural reaction to the mere thought of the beautiful Comtesse de Gremont.

From the moment he'd met her, during her betrothal to Marc, she'd incited his libido. He'd spent a ridiculous amount of time famished for this woman.

Merde. He could make no sense of this incessant, unbreakable pull to her. His desire for her plagued him. Haunted him. The longer it went on, the more it tormented him.

The stronger it got.

So she was beautiful, elegant, graceful, and intelligent. There were others who shared those qualities. So Marc had boasted that his wife was passionate and sensual and highly receptive to his husbandly rights—a woman who saw her marriage bed as enjoyable rather than as a duty. So what? There were other women who enjoyed sex.

He'd fucked scores of them.

Nothing he did got golden-eyed Aimee de Miran out of his head. Out of his system. Not time. Or women. He was tired of wanting her—and worse, comparing other women to her. It drove him to distraction.

Jésus-Christ. He couldn't recall the last time he'd bedded a woman when Aimee hadn't intruded into his mind, where he didn't fantasize it was her he was buried inside.

For the last six years, Adam had kept his distance from Marc's beautiful wife for two reasons. First and foremost, Aimee was in love with her husband, and he never poached where real feelings were involved. Second, Marc was a friend—one who was completely undeserving of his wife's affections. Marc knew full well he'd stirred her heart. He'd laughed about it and found it "adorable," and without discretion of any kind, bedded every woman who crossed his path.

"What about the blue, my lord?"

Adam scrutinized the blue-gray justacorps held out before him.

It was of the finest cloth, yet not boastful. And a fine cut, too. "Perfect."

"I think the lady will be most impressed, my lord." Laurent smiled as he handed him the matching vest—Laurent's usual statement whenever he sensed Adam had a new conquest in mind.

Adam slipped on his vest. "Do you now, Laurent."

"I think you overestimate your charm." Adam could hear the humor in Robert's tone.

He glanced at Robert. "I think you should leave the lady to me and concern yourself with the King, and whether or not he'll approve of our drawings and ideas." Adam slipped on the justacorps with Laurent's assistance.

A member of the Royal Academy of Sciences, he was recognized for his engineering expertise. Over the years, Adam had worked on a number of projects for the Crown—particularly, the fortification of strongholds in case of attack. Now with the country at peace, at least for the time being, Louis had turned his attention to his prized palace.

Versailles.

Unhappy with the water pressure of his fountains, His Majesty had asked Adam to offer a solution to rectify the deficiency the original engineers had produced.

Robert stood and walked over to him, grinning. "It's far more fun watching Adam de Vey fail for the first time with a woman." He placed his hand on Adam's shoulder. "In all seriousness, the lady doesn't much care for either of us. Marc broke her heart. She sees us as being no different than her late husband."

That much he knew.

But Adam wasn't looking for her love. Or to replace Marc in her heart, if he was still there. He was looking for a few hours of shared carnal pleasure. He simply wanted to, no—had to—put an end to this inexplicable mental and physical torment. And there was only one way to kill the longing—and that was to have Aimee every which way he could to sate his lust for her.

Success hinged on his ability to stay focused. Patient. Unfortunately, just as Robert stated, she disliked him.

"I'll succeed," Adam said.

Robert lifted a dark brow. "You're that confident?"

"I am."

A slight smile lifted the corner of Robert's mouth. "Oh, I can't wait to see this. I predict she'll run the other way each time you draw near."

A realistic prediction.

For his sanity's sake, he had to succeed. He couldn't fail. He *would* best her in this cat and mouse game they were about to play. Beautiful, passionate Aimee hadn't had a lover since her Marc's death. He'd left his wife at their country château while he'd carried on with his favorite mistress in the city, and hadn't been anywhere near her for months prior to his fatal duel. In short, she hadn't been touched in a very long time.

And she was ripe for the taking.

Adam was going to use her passionate nature to his advantage.

THANK YOU for reading BEWITCHING IN BOOTS!

Want my next release for just **99¢?** Sign up for my **99¢ New Release Alert** newsletter at www.LilaDiPasqua.com. Each new release will be **99¢** for a SHORT time only. Get notified. Don't miss out!

FIERY TALES SERIES

Novellas
Sleeping Beau
Little Red Writing
Bewitching in Boots
The Marquis's New
Clothes
The Lovely Duckling
The Princess and the
Diamonds

Holiday Novella
The Duke's Match Girl

Anthologies
Awakened by a Kiss
The Princess in His Bed

Full-length novels
A Midnight Dance
Undone
Three Reckless Wishes

Lila DiPasqua is a *USA TODAY* bestselling author of historical romance with heat. She lives with her husband, three children and two rescued dogs and is a firm believer in the happily-ever-after. You can find her on Facebook, Twitter, Instagram, and Goodreads!